A Candlelight Ecstasy Romance™

"MOLLY, . . ." HE WHISPERED. "I DON'T KNOW IF I'LL BE ABLE TO KEEP MY BARGAIN NOT TO TOUCH YOU. . . ."

He raised his head to look at her. He was so close, she could see every little detail of his face, the dark smoldering eyes, the strong nose, the sensual curve of his mouth, the darkened cheekbones, the strong column of his throat.

She saw his mouth, the firm lips slightly parted, then it was against hers, rough and demanding with an insistence that sent her blood thundering through her ears. His hands were moving everywhere, touching her hungrily, urgently. Naked desire mounted in her head, leaving her trembling in his arms. . . .

CANDLELIGHT ECSTASY ROMANCES™

MARRIAGE TO A STRANGER

Dorothy Phillips

A CANDLELIGHT ECSTASY ROMANCE ™

Published by
Dell Publishing Co., Inc.
1 Dag Hammarskjold Plaza
New York, New York 10017

Dell ® TM 681510, Dell Publishing Co., Inc.

Candlelight Ecstasy Romance™ is a trademark of
Dell Publishing Co., Inc., New York, New York.

ISBN: 0–440–15605–X

Printed in the United States of America
First printing—July 1982

Dear Reader:

In response to your continued enthusiasm for Candlelight Ecstasy Romances™, we are increasing the number of new titles from four to six per month.

We are delighted to present sensuous novels set in America, depicting modern American men and women as they confront the provocative problems of modern relationships.

Throughout the history of the Candlelight line, Dell has tried to maintain a high standard of excellence, to give you the finest in reading enjoyment. That is now and will remain our most ardent ambition.

Anne Gisonny
Editor
Candlelight Romances

CHAPTER ONE

The silence in the cabin was deep indeed, deeper than the vast wilderness in which the cabin stood. The man's voice was quiet for a few minutes and the silence pounded against her eardrums. Molly stared at him and vaguely knew he was trying to make it easy for her, but there is no easy way to tell a girl her father is dead. Jim Robinson, bush pilot, and his wife, friends to both Molly and her father, had come to tell her the news before she heard it on the wireless radio. Fortunately the news hadn't reached the remote cabin thirty miles south of Fairbanks. Jim was thankful for that, but the girl was taking the news so calmly, he feared she was in shock.

"Molly?" he said anxiously. Then again, "Molly?"

She looked dully from Jim to his wife, her face blank, uncomprehending. She shifted her gaze, with anguished eyes, to the open doorway and to the lake beyond. Fragments of sunlight leaped and danced gracefully on the blue water and it seemed to Molly that she was suspended in time and space and if she closed her eyes, she could remain there, safe and secure in the life she and her father had made together. She hung in a nondescript void. The silence was as deep and as high as the blue of the sky and the depth of the lake. A memory floated through her mind. Suddenly she recalled her father telling her to be still and listen to the silence. She had not known what he was talking about. Now she knew.

9

Jim took her arms and tugged her toward him, forcing her head down onto his shoulder.

"We never know why these things happen, honey. Why it was Charlie and not one of the other members of the expedition." He realized suddenly that her unnatural calm hid acute bewilderment as well as grief.

The girl's stillness frightened him and he grasped her upper arms and forced her away from him so he could see her face.

"Let it go, Molly!" he said urgently. "Don't hold it inside. It has happened and we can't change it."

"I know. I want to cry, Jim, but it won't . . . come. I loved him so much. I . . . don't know what I'll do without him! No one knew that range like Da—d—Dad. I just can't believe he could fall in a crevice!" The tears came. Big racking sobs shook the small body that Jim held against him. She cried tears of despair. Her voice, sobbing and tremulous in anguish, called to her father over and over again. The big man could do nothing but hold her while his wife stood by helplessly, her own eyes swimming in tears.

After awhile the sobbing ceased and Molly raised her wet, swollen eyes to Jim.

"Evelyn will stay with you," he said gently. "Her mother will take care of our boys."

"Thank you." Her voice held a queerly resigned note which Jim found far more pathetic than her tears. "I'll be all right now, but if you will excuse me, I'd like to be alone for a while." Her unwavering glance held his. "I'm sorry, Jim, for making it so hard for you to tell me." He touched her head with clumsy tenderness.

They watched her leave the room; head bowed, shoulders slumped as though the weight of the world rested upon them. She had retreated once again into the deep recesses of her own reserve and Jim shook his head as he heard the door of her bedroom close softly.

10

Evelyn looked anxiously at her husband.

"What will she do, Jim?"

"I don't know, but as much as Charlie loved that girl, I'm sure he must have considered the possibility that she could be left alone. He knew these expeditions were dangerous, although he never let Molly know. He cautioned me more than once not to mention it to her."

He sighed and pulled his wife down beside him on the couch. They sat for a few minutes without speaking. Both turned their heads toward the bedroom door, but no sound came from beyond. If Molly insisted on wrapping herself away in that impenetrable reserve of hers, there was little they could do for her; they could only wait and hope that by staying near she was comforted.

Jim looked down at his wife and saw that although she had leaned her head back against the couch and closed her eyes, big tears were creeping down under her lashes and trickling unheeded down her cheeks.

"Evelyn!"

She opened her eyes and he saw mirrored there all the sorrow and compassion her generous heart felt for her friend. With an exclamation he leaned forward and gathered her up in his arms. They sat quietly together for a long while before Evelyn broke the silence.

"Do you think she'll go to Anchorage, Jim? She has never talked much about the time she spent with Charlie's sister, but I got the impression she wasn't happy there."

"I don't know if she will go to Anchorage or not. I do know she can't stay here alone. Good Lord! It's ten miles to the nearest neighbor. She may be twenty-five years old, but she's as innocent as a babe. Every single man within a hundred miles will be finding an excuse to come by here."

"And a few that are not single," Evelyn asserted dryly. "She's been here with Charlie for about six years, hasn't she?"

11

"Ever since she left the convent school, except for the few months she spent in the city with Charlie's sister. Charlie taught her a lot about how to take care of herself, or he wouldn't have left her here alone for a week or two at a time. Of course Tim-Two was here to look out for her while he was away."

"I forgot all about the Indian. You'll have to tell him."

"Yes, I know. He's been with Charlie for a long time. He came here one winter about half starved to death. Charlie took him in, and he's been here ever since. I haven't any idea how old he is, but I imagine he would be a pretty wicked enemy."

Evelyn laughed softly. "Just to look at him scares me. That one eye of his that goes off in the other direction gives me the willies!"

Jim stood up. "I'll go talk to him. Make some coffee, will you, honey? I think we should leave Molly alone for a while. She'll come out and talk when she's ready."

He went through the kitchen and out the back door toward a cabin that was set about a hundred feet behind the house. Tim-Two had built the cabin himself. It was small, tight, and really quite ugly, like the man himself.

Evelyn busied herself about the kitchen. She stoked up the big wood range and set the granite coffeepot on to perk. She looked around the neat room. Nicely built cabinets lined one wall, with a stainless steel sink set into the middle of the counter top. A hand water pump was perched on one end of the sink. The big cooking range dominated the opposite wall; shiny black, with touches of blue on the big oven door at the bottom and on the doors of the two warming ovens at the top. The hot water reservoir was on one side of the range and the woodbox on the other.

She sat down at the trestle table that divided the kitchen from the living room, and let her gaze wander over the cozily furnished room. A stone fireplace, big enough to

12

accommodate a six-foot-long log, took up the entire end of the room. In this cold country heating was a main concern, and heat from the fireplace and the cooking range in the kitchen kept the rooms comfortably warm. Evelyn knew too, about the potbellied stoves in each of the two bedrooms. There was a rocking chair on one side of the fireplace and a comfortable pillow-lined couch on the other side. In between the two was a bright braided rug. The pillows, curtains, Charlie's pipe on the table, all caught Evelyn's eye as she looked about the room. Molly had done a good job turning this old barn of a cabin into a home; not fancy by city standards, but very comfortable. The girl was a natural homemaker, no doubt about that. It was unfair that she would have to leave it all.

Molly lay on the bed in her room, arms under her head, dazed eyes focused on the ceiling. Dry eyed, now, thinking about the big, burly dark-haired man that was her father. When her mother died, the nature of her father's work had forced him to make arrangements for her to be cared for in a convent school. From the age of six her life had been regulated by the strict nuns. When she reached the age of eighteen, she had about decided to enter the cloister because she knew of no other kind of life. Disturbed about the step she was considering, Charlie took her out of the convent and brought her to Anchorage to live with his sister. He wanted her to have a taste of living in the outside world before she turned her back on it forever.

Molly endured the time she spent with Aunt Dora and her cousins like a prison sentence. Fashion and the social life of Anchorage was their life and from the beginning she had felt oddly out of place in their home. After two months she longed for the quiet of the convent and begged Charlie to let her go back there if he didn't want her to share his home in the bush. The happiest day of her life was when she packed her things and Charlie loaded them in his old pickup truck and headed north. That was almost six years ago and Molly could count on one hand the times she had been to the city since then.

Charlie had been afraid that the wild north country would be lonely for his only child, but she took to the life like a duck to water. Her natural instinct for making a home exerted itself and she plunged into the work with vigor. The first few months she scrubbed, cleaned, painted, and hung pictures. She made curtains and slipcovers for the couch and chairs. The delighted Charlie let her have full reign of the house and was constantly amazed at all she could do. The sisters at the school had trained her well in the art of cooking, as Charlie discovered to his pleasure, and he wondered how he had ever gotten along without her.

Lying there on the bed Molly thought about the love her father had for his work and that now he would never finish the job he had started. He loved Alaska and spent many evenings discussing with her the potential of the country. He was the country's foremost authority on ice age mammals, and his research had taken him to every part of the great Alaskan tundra. What would happen to his work now that he was gone? He had colleagues, but Molly had met few of them. He mentioned their names from time to time, but she didn't think he worked closely with them because he preferred to work, for the most part, alone. She wondered if she should contact one of them and offer her father's files. Well—she would have to think about that for a while.

She gave a deep, dejected sigh and slipped off the bed. Many things would have to be decided, but not now. There would not be a funeral service for her father, but a memorial service would be held later on and she supposed she would have Aunt Dora to contend with and she wasn't looking forward to that.

Glancing about the room Molly caught her reflection in the mirror and was surprised she looked no different than

14

she had yesterday after all that had happened. The outside of her was still the same, but the inside was totally different. She wondered if anyone else in the world felt as empty as she did.

Having no exalted opinion of herself Molly was completely unaware of her beauty, although she realized she was prettier than some girls. A few of the men that had come to call on her cousins had looked at her in a friendly way, but her shyness had prevented her from making friends with any of them. Her cousins hadn't seemed anxious for her to mix socially with the crowd they ran with. This hadn't bothered her for they all seemed to be quite frivolous.

Jim and Evelyn were sitting at the trestle table when Molly came out of the bedroom. *What a totally feminine girl she is,* thought Evelyn. Her small five-foot three-inch body was slim but softly rounded. She was an elfen-type girl who moved lightly on the ground as if her feet were skimming the surface. The honey-colored hair hung almost to her waist and she wore it now in one long, loose braid hanging down her back. Occasionally she wore it in a neat braid on top of her head and it made her look like a small girl playing dress-up. Violet eyes, rimmed with dark lashes, were set into a face that had known very little makeup. Her good health gave her the soft, clear skin and the slight rosiness to her cheeks. She had no vanity about her eyes or the soft mouth that was quick to tilt into a smile. Molly Develon was a very pretty girl; not only pretty on the outside but on the inside, as well. Being shy and sweet-natured, she would never knowingly offend anyone.

Evelyn jumped up and went to the range. "Sit down, Molly, I'll get you some coffee. Jim will be leaving in a few minutes."

She set the coffee cup in front of Molly and went around

15

the table to sit on the long bench beside her husband. He put his arm around her and she snuggled close.

"Don't think you need to stay with me, Evelyn. I've been here alone many times." Molly's voice was soft but controlled.

"I'm staying and that's the end of it," Evelyn said firmly.

"Of course she's staying. I'll get all the more lovin' when she comes back to me." Jim's attempt at light banter brought a smile to his wife's face.

"Don't let him fool you, Molly. He gets his share of lovin'."

"Yes, I know, and I do appreciate you doing this for me."

Jim reached across and took Molly's hand. "Molly, there isn't a person south of Fairbanks who wouldn't have broken their necks to do something for you. You've endeared yourself to all of us. We all want to help, you have only to ask." Tears came to her eyes, she swallowed the lump in her throat, but said nothing. "If you agree," Jim continued, "I'll arrange a memorial service for Charlie day after tomorrow. Herb Belsile, Charlie's attorney, and I will take care of everything."

"That's kind of you," Molly murmured. "Perhaps you will notify Aunt Dora in Anchorage?"

"Sure. Now . . . there are a few things I would like to say before I go," Jim said kindly. "Herb will be out in about a week to see you. He knows Evelyn will be staying here with you and he seems to think he should come out here rather than you going into the city to see him. I don't have any idea what provisions Charlie made for you. Herb will have to tell you that. But Molly, honey, you can't stay out here alone this winter." He paused and Molly's heart gave a queer little jerk. "What I'm trying to say is this. In the next few days try and get yourself in the frame of mind to accept whatever Herb has to tell you. Charlie will have

16

left you financially secure, but he wouldn't have wanted you to stay here alone."

Molly's breath caught and she stared at him. It hadn't occurred to her that she wouldn't stay here; this was her home.

She said, with a catch in her voice, "I love this place. I don't want to leave it. The happiest years of my life were spent here."

"You'll have to be practical, honey. It would be dangerous for you to spend the winter here alone."

"I'll have Tim-Two and if Dad left me money, I'll hire someone to come and stay with me. I have the citizen's band radio and the snowmobile."

"You're very capable, Molly, but think of this. A lovely young girl here alone, miles from anyone except an Indian of undetermined age. While Tim-Two is devoted to you, and would defend you with his life, it's still too great a risk for you to take. The ratio of men to girls in this area is about ten to one, and the ratio of pretty young girls to men is greater than that. Men from miles around will be dropping by when they learn you are here alone, and some of them could be pretty obnoxious. Think about it, Molly." He smiled at her and squeezed her hands. "Let's don't worry about it now. You know Evelyn and I would be happy to have you with us, that is, if you could stand two wild Indians ages four and six."

"Thank you, Jim. I know you're thinking of what is best for me, but try to understand. This is the only home I've ever known and if I must leave it, it won't make the slightest difference where I go . . . Anchorage, Fairbanks, or New York City. My heart is here." Molly looked up, her violet eyes bright with unshed tears. "Until I came here, I had spent my life in a convent school except for the two months with Aunt Dora. I don't think I could bear to leave this place. I love the tall pines, the spring flowers,

17

the snow, the wildlife, and my dog. I could never take Dog to the city, Jim. I'll do anything to stay here!"

Jim sighed and told her he understood how she felt. He didn't realize it at the time, but in the next few weeks he would remember those words: "I'll do anything to stay here."

After Jim took his leave, the women sat quietly, listening to the sound of the motor as the plane circled the house and headed back to Fairbanks.

Molly sat in the rocking chair by the fireplace, the chair she occupied most evenings. Evelyn found herself busy answering calls on the battery-powered radio. The news about Charlie was out and it seemed everyone within radio range wanted to offer their condolences. Molly heard Evelyn say over and over again, "Thank you so much, but . . . no, I don't think she needs anything. Yes, I will tell her. I'll be staying with her for a while. Jim will be getting in touch with you regarding the service. Thank you, I'll give her the message. No she hasn't made any plans."

How thankful she was for Evelyn. Molly sat and rocked. Her thoughts raced. *Dad . . . how I'll miss you. We had such a short time together. What will I ever do without you? I must not feel sorry for myself; I must think clearly and figure out a way to stay here in my home. If only I could find someone to stay with me, but not many people want to spend a winter in an isolated place such as this. It will be lonesome here without you, Dad, but not as lonesome as it would be if I were in the city . . .*"

Hearing a faint scratching sound, Evelyn opened the kitchen door to admit a large shaggy dog. He walked across the room to where Molly sat in the rocking chair and laid his head in her lap. He looked up into her face with large adoring eyes. She reached out her hand and stroked his head.

"Hello, Dog," she said softly. "You'll miss him too, won't you, fellow?"

The back door opened once again and the Indian, Tim-Two, came noiselessly into the kitchen. He checked the water reservoir on the cooking range, then the big wood-box beside the stove. He placed several armloads of neatly cut logs by the fireplace, then knelt and built up the fire. The evenings in the north woods were cool. The Indian didn't look at Molly; he seldom did. As he passed her chair he placed a hand lightly on top of her head and she knew he had been told about her father. He had never touched her before. Tears came again to her eyes and at that moment she felt closer to that old Indian man than to anyone else in the world.

CHAPTER TWO

Always, in the Alaskan country, there is the wildlife. Virtually no day passed without a succession of wild creatures coming within viewing distance of the house. They had been a constant source of delight to Molly; the deer, elk, moose, sly fox, porcupines, and the black and grizzly bears that lived in the valley.

Molly's Siberian husky, fondly called Dog, never seemed to learn that he made the porcupines nervous and after more than one encounter came home bristling. Molly kept a pair of pliers handy for pulling out the quills. She liked to think Dog was smarter about frightening off the black or grizzly bears, a potential hazard in the summer. Usually, the bears were looking for food and probably wouldn't bother you, but Charlie had warned her of the danger and she would scurry into the house or take refuge in the woodshed when one came near. Dog would dash back and forth, keeping his distance, barking ferociously until the bear, tired of the racket, went on its way.

Their land, bordering a twenty-acre lake, lay alongside the right-of-way of a highway that came south out of Fairbanks. The highway was a mile from the house and the railway a half a mile beyond that. In the summer supplies were brought in on the floatplane that landed on the lake eighty yards from the house. During the winter months they came by rail or ski plane. Orders were mailed or sent via the wireless radio to Fairbanks or to Anchorage and when the store had filled the order and was ready to send it, they would broadcast the news over a daily radio program of personal messages for people living in the outlying areas. Listening to this program was also a good way to keep up with the local happenings. When they heard, "freight for Develons leaving tomorrow," Charlie, Tim-Two, and sometimes Molly would head for the rail line where the freight would be dropped. The trip was made by skis, snowshoes, dogsled, or snowmobile, whichever the load demanded. Charlie kept a four-wheel drive vehicle in a shed along the highway, but the uncertainty of getting the motor started and road conditions made that means of transportation unreliable.

Snow cover lasted from October until May or early June. Winter was a lonely time, especially during the coldest spells. The vast area around the cabin would seem lifeless except for the birds. The gray jays and the gay little chickadees would find their way to Molly's feeder and would scold noisily when it was empty. The small, furry animals kept out of sight, burrowed deep in the snow, coming out only when their empty stomachs demanded food.

In the evenings, when it was cold and dark and the wind was howling, Molly or her father would stoke up the fire in the huge fireplace and put a record on the battery-powered stereo and listen to Beethoven, Bach, or, occasionally, to a Nelson Eddy ballad about the frozen North. With the records and plenty of fresh reading material Molly and Charlie had been content.

In the winter the moose would move out of the hills into the woods about the cabin. During the hunting season Tim-Two would shoot a good sized one to be butchered for the winter supply of meat. Hanging the carcass in the woodshed, the below zero temperature would keep the meat, and from it Molly would cook delicious steaks, roasts, and stews.

In summer, with the snow gone, the long daylight hours would bring a frenzy of activity. Tim-Two would replenish the wood supply, and you could hear the ringing of the ax and the buzz of the chain saw for days. Molly would get the "berry picking fever" and collect blueberries, raspberries, cranberries, and currants. She would make fresh pies and cobblers as well as can countless jars of jams and jellies.

Being out in the woods in Alaska in the summer meant having to contend with the pesky mosquito, but they soon got used to covering themselves with insect repellent before leaving the house.

It was a lovely way of life and Molly wanted no other. She wanted to live the rest of her life here in this house in this valley. Like all girls she had dreamed of falling in love, but in her dreams the husband and children lived with her here in this place.

Jim came for Molly and Evelyn the day of the memorial service for Charlie. Landing the floatplane on the lake they boarded from the small dock Tim-Two had put in for that purpose and for Molly to use for fishing. The trip and the service were an ordeal for Molly. Not being used to meeting people she found it difficult to greet and respond to her father's many friends who came forward to speak to her. Knowing she was being observed she kept her head down and her eyes dry holding her grief until the time she would be alone.

Strangely Aunt Dora posed no problems, probably thinking Molly was of age and she would no longer need be concerned with her.

Jim suggested that Molly spend the night at their home in the city. Molly consented to this knowing how much Evelyn wanted to be with Jim and the boys. However, no amount of talking could persuade her from returning to the cabin in the bush.

For the next few days Molly tried to put Herb Belsile's

visit out of her mind. Although she kept the house spotless most of the time, she and Evelyn went over it together and the task kept Molly's mind busy as well as her hands. They made repairs on Molly's limited wardrobe and sewed several shirts for Evelyn's boys.

When Molly thought about it, she chided herself for her lack of faith that her father would provide her with the means of staying in her home. Knowing how he loved her, she was sure he had made arrangements that would make it possible . . . and yet the anxiety struggled painfully in the back of her mind, and even that was partially blocked out by her overwhelming desire that, in spite of all the reasons Jim had given her for leaving, she would stay.

On the morning of the attorney's visit the house was filled with the delicious aroma of fresh baked bread and apple pie.

Evelyn laughingly said, "Jim will follow his nose right to the house."

With beef roast and potatoes in the oven, Molly took time to freshen up before their guest arrived. She bathed her face and slipped on a soft blue blouse and matching skirt. She wrapped her shining braids around her head and slipped her feet into slim heeled pumps. On an impulse she applied a touch of lipstick to her lips. "Dutch courage," she told herself. With that thought, she turned back to dab a small amount of perfume to the base of her throat. She wanted this meeting to be over as she had never wanted anything else since the whimsical desires of her childhood. It was ridiculous, of course, because her father would have planned what he thought was best for her. She could almost hear his reassuring voice saying, "It will be all right."

Jim's voice was coming in on the citizen's band radio. "KGF-1452 . . . calling KFK-1369 . . . come in, Evie baby. Your ever-lovin's callin' . . ."

Grinning, Evelyn picked up the microphone. "Jim, you idiot, everyone within fifty miles is listening!"

"Ten-four, Evie baby," Jim's voice came back. "What's wrong with them all knowing I'm your ever-lovin'?"

"Nothing at all, but the radio is supposed to be used for business and not for . . . horsin' around."

"Yes, I know. You are my business, Evie baby. See you in a few . . . KGF-1452 mobile down and clear."

Molly heard the plane go over the cabin and a few minutes later it landed on the lake. The girls threw light sweaters over their shoulders and went out onto the porch.

Jim was striding purposefully up the path. Molly was surprised to see two men following Jim. She knew the shorter, heavier man was Herb Belsile, her father's attorney. The other man was some distance away, but Molly was sure she didn't know him and guessed he was one of Herb's assistants.

Herb approached Molly, holding out his hand. "Hello, Molly. I'm sorry we are meeting under these circumstances. Please accept my deepest sympathy. Charlie was one of my best friends."

"Thank you, Herb." Molly gave him her hand. "Do you know, Mrs. Robinson, Jim's wife? She has been kind enough to spend a few days with me."

Evelyn was standing in Jim's embrace, but extended her hand to Herb.

"Nice meeting you, Mr. Belsile. Molly and I hope you men are hungry. We've been cooking up a storm."

The third man had not come forward to be introduced. He was standing back, feet braced apart, staring at Molly. He was casually dressed in tan twill pants and a tan and green ski sweater. Molly looked at him and thought him handsome. He was looking directly at her and she couldn't look away. His eyes were luminous black, and like his mouth were just there in his face, grave, quiet, and bitter. They remained on her and Molly found herself caught in

24

a silent waiting game with him. Slowly those shining, bitter eyes looked her over from the crown of her head to the tips of her shoes, and back to her face. Her eyes flicked up warily and she looked straight in the dark fire of his eyes. His mouth went colder and he nodded his head in greeting, against his will, or so it seemed.

Molly held her breath until her chest hurt, then breathed deeply when his eyes left her. He had measured her with his eyes for some purpose known only to himself, had estimated her, and found her lacking. A tightness crept into her throat. She merely stood there, hands at her sides, endeavoring not to clench her fingers with nervousness. He was the type of man to judge one on first impressions, she decided, with a mental sigh. At least it seemed to her that was what he was doing, because his dark face was wearing a positively thundercloud look.

Herb was talking to Jim and Evelyn so Molly stole another look at the man. He was tall, very tall, with a broadness to go with it. He had dark hair that curled down on the collar of the turtleneck sweater he wore. He had a dark face, a tight jaw, and a bleak mouth. *He doesn't like me,* she thought suddenly, *and how foolish of me to care.* With that she turned back to Herb.

"Oh, Molly," he said, "this is Adam Reneau."

Molly glanced at the man and nodded, but did not offer her hand. She turned from him and led her guests into the house.

Jim kept up a lively conversation with Evelyn while they set the meal on the table. Occasionally Molly glanced at the man. She had a feeling his eyes missed nothing as he looked around the room. An uneasy feeling came over her that this stranger was assessing her home. Something akin to panic made her heart pound and she felt a compelling urgency to get this day behind her.

During the meal Molly made little contribution to the general conversation. She was content to listen as voices echoed around and above her. She kept her eyes on her plate and tried not to look at Adam. The one time she let herself look at him she found the dark eyes watching her intently without much expression in them. Her chin tilted slightly and she said with a cool dignity that surprised her:

"Would you like some pie, Mr. Reneau?"

"Yes, please." His voice sounded equally cool.

She served him silently, determined not to speak to him again unless it was absolutely necessary.

"Very good pie, ladies," Herb said. "Very good. Don't you think so, Adam?"

"It's delicious, Mrs. Robinson." His voice was deep and soft, not at all the tone he had used with Molly.

"Oh, I can't take any of the credit." Evelyn gestured with her fork. "Molly baked the pies."

"Is that so," he said dryly, making it a statement and not a question.

"Oh, my, yes!" Evelyn rambled on. "Molly can cook circles around me any day. Charlie was proud as punch at the way Molly could cook. Why—" Suddenly she was aware she was embarrassing Molly when the color came up to flood her face.

"Is that so?" Adam Reneau said again flatly.

"Well, now . . ." Herb started to stand up.

"Sit right here," Evelyn insisted. "I'll clear off these dishes. You'll have plenty of room to spread out your papers and things. Jim and I have things to talk about. We'll take Mr. Reneau out and show him around."

"That's kind of you, Mrs. Robinson, but Adam will have to stay. What I have to tell Molly also concerns him."

Molly's eyes flew to Herb's face. Her future having something to do with this cold man? *Impossible! And if Herb thinks he's going to turn my affairs over to this . . . man, I'll soon straighten him out about that.* She blinked, opened her mouth to say something, but thought

26

better of it after one quick glance at that horrible man's disgusted expression. She compressed her lips and cleared the dishes from the table and carried them to the sink. When she returned, she sat down at the table opposite Herb. Adam Reneau took the chair at the end of the table between the two of them.

Herb got out his briefcase and piled papers on the table. He shuffled them around several times. It seemed to Molly he was ill at ease. He cleared his throat while going through the papers and beads of perspiration popped out on his brow. He was definitely uncomfortable and Molly's anxiety grew.

"Molly," he said at last. "Adam already knows the contents of your father's will and that is the reason he came here with me to explain it to you. But first, I want you to know, I did everything I could to talk Charlie out of this plan. When he first brought the idea to me six months ago, I told him then I thought it was an out and out hairbrained scheme. Although, I can understand, to a certain extent, why he did it, even if you and Adam won't." His voice took on a pleading note. "He loved you more than anything else in the world, Molly. After you, he loved his work. I think he thought that by bringing you and Adam together he was doing his best for both you and his work."

"What does he want me to do?" It was strange and frightening to ask the question.

Her face was so full of anguish Herb's heart went out to her. He placed his hands over hers on the table and said as kindly as he could: "Your father wants you to marry Adam."

The surprise of his statement took her so completely, she went white and stared at him in terrible silence. Her body went rigid, her face set. Her lips moved, shook, and fell apart.

"I don't believe it . . . Dad wouldn't!"

Her tortured eyes turned to Adam. Resentment. It was there in the grim line of his jaw and in the bitter unsmiling eyes. He leaned back in his chair, his grim face tight.

"It wasn't my idea, Miss Develon." The mockingly drawled words were like a slap in the face.

"Wait a minute, Adam," Herb said firmly. "Let me explain things to her."

"Explain away, Herb, but I want her to know, straight off, that I don't want to marry her. A year, six months, a woman never lets go once she gets a legal hold on you. You could figure a way out of this for me if you would set your mind to it."

"I tried, Adam. This will is ring tight and Charlie had the right to do as he wished with his property."

"Charlie knew how badly I wanted to work on this project or he would have never thought up this idiotic scheme."

"I know." Herb spoke as patiently as if he were speaking to a child. "But in all fairness to Molly, she didn't know of his plans."

"I'm not so sure. Women go to great lengths these days to get a rich husband."

"Adam, really! Why don't you leave us and let me talk to Molly alone?"

"Not on your life! I'm staying! This concerns me and I'm going to hear every bit of it." He turned his dark eyes on Molly. With the faintest suggestion of a sardonic smile on his face, he settled back and folded his arms, as if that was his final word.

This can't be happening to me, this can't be happening to me . . . the words ran through Molly's mind over and over again. *They are talking about me is if I'm not here, as if my opinion counts for nothing. Well, I can set that man's mind to rest. I wouldn't marry him if he were the last man on earth. He's the most annoying, hateful, egotistical person I've ever met.*

Herb looked at his old friend's daughter's flushed face. She was a beautiful girl, twenty-five years old with the youthful look of innocence. Adam was a lucky man. She could have been ugly and dull. Herb felt a pang of compassion for her. This unsophisticated girl was no mate for the hard, experienced man sitting beside her. Almost ten years her senior, with more money than he could spend, plus his good looks, he was a prime target for designing females out on the prowl for a husband. This could account for his bitter outlook on life. Everyone that came in contact with him wanted something. Charlie Develon must have known him well and had plenty of confidence in him to trust him with his lovely daughter. A lot could happen in a year. Herb sighed and turned to the girl. He had to try and make her understand that her father had done what he thought was best for her.

"Your father came to see me about a year ago, Molly. He was disturbed about your future. His heart wasn't in the best condition, but that wasn't what troubled him. He desperately wanted to go on this expedition he had planned for so long. Knowing there was a certain amount of risk attached to the trip, added to the fact his heart wasn't as sound as it should be, he wanted to find a way to make your future secure." Herb paused and reshuffled his papers.

"The fortune he left you is considerable. Not a huge amount, but enough for you to live comfortably. What bothered him was the attachment you had formed for this house and this valley. I'm aware of your childhood and how you spent it and can understand the feeling you have for this house. Charlie was hoping he would live to see you married with children of your own." He paused and shifted around in his chair, watching Molly with worried eyes.

Her heart contracted painfully at the thought of her father carrying this burden of concern for her and she bit her lips to stop their trembling.

Herb continued, "Charlie realized that if anything should happen to him, you wouldn't be able to stay here alone. He didn't want you to stay here alone. He was clear in his instructions about that."

Molly started to protest, but Herb waved her silent and glanced at Adam.

"This is what Charlie wanted you to do, Molly." His voice became stronger and took on a professional tone. "Charlie wanted you to marry Adam and live here in this house with him for one year. At the end of that time you can divorce Adam if you wish, and I can turn your money over to you and you can do as you want. You can live here alone or you can hire someone to live with you. You may wish to build some cabins around the lake, and turn this beautiful area into a hunting and fishing lodge, or you may want to sell it and go to the city." Herb took a deep breath. "Let me finish. I need to tell you what to expect if you do not choose to marry Adam. In case you and Adam do not marry . . . ," he looked nervously at Adam, who was looking intently at the kitchen range, "your Aunt Dora will have the control of your money for five years."

The expression on Molly's face might have been amusing had the circumstances been otherwise. She looked positively stunned. She stared at Herb as if he were a man from outer space, and seemed totally incapable of speech.

"Why? Why did he do this to me?" She was surprised to hear that her voice was so calm and even . . . and then not surprised, because a kind of cold numbing chill was gripping her heart, killing all feeling. "Why, Herb? Why did he want me to marry this . . . stranger, and why does this stranger feel he is being forced to marry me?"

"In the first place, Molly," Herb said after a pause, "Adam was no stranger to Charlie, and Charlie didn't plan to leave you so soon. His intentions were to have Adam come out here to help him with his work and for you two to get acquainted. Now, in answer to your second question. Adam is a biologist and is working on the adaption of living things to hostile environments and there are few environments as hostile as the Alaskan tundra. It would set Adam's research ahead five years if he had access to your father's files. Charlie knew this and planned to bring Adam in to work with him, but knowing his time might be cut short he made these . . . other arrangements. His plan was for you and Adam to marry and live here for a year. You would be in the home you love and Adam would have his files to carry on his studies."

Adam's chair scraped the floor and he let out a snort of disgust. Herb gave him a slightly displeased look.

"I want to finish, if you don't mind, Adam. You know the rest, but Molly does not, so please be patient a little longer. Molly, your father has arranged for me to have the files destroyed if Adam refuses to marry you."

The words fell like a bombshell against Molly's ears. It was incredible to her that her father would consider destroying his files, his life's work. He always said his files were his contribution to society.

Herb was talking again and Molly brought herself back with an effort to hear what he was saying.

"I'm going to leave you two alone so you can decide what to do. You know the alternatives. Keep in mind the fact that Charlie knew you both very well and spent many hours carefully planning each detail of his will. I have a personal letter from him to give each of you. Think about what you want and what you have to lose if you decide to refuse the terms of the will. When you've made your decision, call me. I'll be on the porch." He took two sealed envelopes from his briefcase and handed the first one to Molly, the second to Adam. Then he left them.

Molly looked at the letter in her hand. Tears flooded her eyes so she could hardly see her name on the envelope. She stood up, but kept her face averted from Adam. With trembling lips and with as much dignity as she could muster, she said, "Excuse me for a few minutes."

He got to his feet. "Certainly."

With head up and back straight she walked to her bedroom door on shaky legs. In the privacy of her room she allowed the tears to course down her cheeks unchecked. She cried softly, as a deer cries when wounded, or a very small animal when caught in a trap. Her tears splashed down on the envelope she still held tightly in her hand. The awareness of the loss of her father was more acute now than any time since the accident. Horrified at her lack of control, she took a tissue from her bedside table and wiped her eyes and blew her nose. After a few minutes she was composed enough to open the envelope. With trembling fingers she unfolded the single sheet and began to read.

> My Darling Molly,
>
> Herb will have told you of my plan for you before he gave you this letter. I hope, with all my heart, that you will marry Adam. He is a good man. He needs a girl like you and you need a strong man like him. I know him well and trust him. He is the type of man who will appreciate a home such as you and I have enjoyed these past years. He will take care of you for a year and at the end of that time you will be able to decide for yourself the direction your life will take. Don't be angry with me, my Molly. Trust me. I am trying to grab some happiness for you.
>
> Your loving Dad

Molly reread the letter several times, returned it to the envelope, and slipped it into the drawer of her nightstand. She didn't understand the last sentence. "Grab some happiness" . . . Did he think she would be happy with that man out there? Poor Dad. He didn't leave her much choice. She had never known her father to make a hasty judgment or an uncalculated decision. In spite of her dislike for the man she would marry him, if he agreed. A year wasn't really so long, considering the alternative.

CHAPTER THREE

A calm and composed girl went back into the living room. Adam had moved from the chair by the table to the couch by the fireplace and lounged there, his head resting against the back, seemingly lost in thought. He stood up when Molly came into the room. She didn't see any sign of the letter Herb had given him from her father. Somehow she had expected to see it in his hand. He waited for her to sit down and indicated the chair opposite the couch, but Molly wanted to be standing on her feet when she told him what she had to say. She tilted her head so she could look him straight in the eye.

"Mr. Reneau." Her voice was calm and controlled. "I'm sorry you've been put in this uncomfortable position. If I had the authority, I would turn my father's files over to you so you could finish your research, but as you know, I can't do that. It would break my heart to see his life's work destroyed. I'm willing to marry you, for a year, if it's agreeable with you."

By the time she had finished her speech she was almost breathless from the effort of trying to maintain her calm, and her last words almost faded away as they left her trembling lips.

"It didn't take you long to decide. Are you sure you are willing to marry this . . . stranger? Can it be you have discovered I am a wealthy man and that's the reason for your change of mind?" His voice was edged with a sneer and his hard black eyes probed hers.

"Think what you like. It may be hard for you to believe this, but there are some things more important than money . . . and if you are suggesting—"

"Hadn't it occurred to you?" he broke in rudely.

"No, it had not occurred to me." Her anger made her voice louder and sharper than she had intended. "And— and I'll tell you one thing, Mr. Reneau. If we agree to this . . . er . . . arrangement, I'll ask Herb to draw up a contract to the effect you'll have no financial responsibility for me . . . ever! I'll insist on this!"

She was amazed at her temerity to say such a thing, but she was glad. It might be just as well to show him from the beginning that she had no intention of allowing him to bully her, especially since this marriage was just as advantageous to him as it was to her.

Adam raised his dark brows. "Shall we sit down, Miss Develon?"

Molly sat in the rocking chair and Adam returned to the couch. There was a brief pause of silence before he spoke.

"You realize, of course, if we agree to this contract, it will be an impersonal relationship and at the end of the year we will get the marriage annulled, which is much simpler than a divorce. It will only hinge on the results of a doctor's examination . . . of you. You are a virgin?"

He felt a sharp stab of pleasure as the color came up and flooded her face, then a tinge of regret, for he knew this girl had not the cosmopolitan veneer of the women he usually associated with. The thought crossed his mind that it had been quite awhile since he had seen a woman blush.

Determined not to let him put her down, Molly tilted her head and looked straight into his amused eyes.

"Of course," she said matter-of-factly, then added; "I

35

wouldn't even consider anything but an impersonal relationship . . . with you, Mr. Reneau."

Adam laughed out loud as the blush burned brightly in her cheeks. "You think not?" he said softly, perfectly aware of the fury that was making her speechless. He lounged back against the couch, his arms crossed over his chest, a speculative gleam in his dark eyes.

Unable to continue staring at his mocking face without losing her temper, Molly dropped her gaze and watched her fingers intently for a moment as they aimlessly pleated the material of her skirt. The silence became heavy. The only sounds being the voices coming faintly from the porch as Jim talked with Herb. Adam continued to observe her, quietly and openly.

Molly squirmed inwardly. She felt a desperate desire to get this business over and settled. She hesitated, biting her lips in spite of her self-control.

"Well . . . have you decided . . . ?"

"Have I decided to marry you?" He finally spoke, although he waited so long Molly was not sure he was going to answer. "Yes, I decided to marry you as soon as I read Charlie's will." His dark eyes raked her face searchingly, while remaining inscrutable themselves. "If you had been fat, bald, and with a mustache, I still would marry you. The fact that you're young, beautiful, and obviously a good cook, is a bonus I didn't expect."

Molly was conscious of that dark, unreadable scrutiny and an icy chill crept through her body.

"You are that desperate to use my father's files?" It was a stated fact.

"Yes," he said, not taking his eyes from hers.

"I see." Molly resisted the absurd desire to giggle childishly. "People will have to know that this marriage between us is a business arrangement."

"I have no wish, myself, that it should become public knowledge. At the present only Herb and myself are aware

36

of the conditions of the will—besides yourself, of course. The Robinsons will guess, and have to be told, but we can trust their discretion, I'm sure."

Molly stiffened. The idea of any kind of pretended married affinity between herself and Adam Reneau was ridiculous. Surely he wasn't suggesting such a thing.

"What do you propose we do?" Carefully she controlled her voice so that it sounded cool and businesslike. She found herself looking at him with personal eyes, feeling a shock at discovering that he was so very attractive, that she could like him if only he were not so cold and withdrawn.

"After our marriage I'll take you to meet my father. This marriage will make two fathers happy, yours and mine. My father is eighty-four years old. I am the result of his one and only love affair. He married late in life and he wants to see me happily married before I reach middle age. This is very important to him and I insist he be made to believe my marriage is as happy and fulfilling for me as his was for him. We will spend a few days with him after the wedding and give him the impression that we enjoy a normal, loving marriage. Afterwards, when the time comes for the annulment, if my father is still living, we will simply tell him the marriage didn't work out. I don't believe he will ever have to be told since at present his health is so poor."

Adam leaned back on the couch watching her all the time. His expression was as unreadable as ever. His thoughts raced ahead to the time he would present his wife to his father. She would be perfect for the part. The inscrutable mask of his expression broke slightly, one dark brow lifted, and his dark eyes glinted with amusement.

"Do you think you can comply with the terms?"

"Terms?" She gave him a startled look.

"Can you pretend to be in love with me?"

Surprise made the color come quickly back to her face.

She didn't dare look at him. Instead she stared down at her hands clenched in her lap. Inwardly she quaked and shrank from the thought of deceiving an old man—but so much was at stake!

"Would it be so hard to do?" There was a tight smile on his mouth, and Molly thought she could hear a trace of a challenge in his voice.

There was a shocking little silence, and it seemed to drag on for hours before she could say anything. Finally, the violet eyes looked directly into the pitless dark ones and she said in a low voice.

"The terms are . . . acceptable."

"Good." He got to his feet. "Now, I'd like to see your father's study and look over the place where I'll spend the next year of my life."

Molly said nothing, but led the way to her father's combination study and bedroom.

The house had originally been built of rough logs, but in later years insulation and an inner wall had been added. One side of the square cabin was taken up with living room and kitchen; the two bedrooms and bath were in the other half. The elimination of a hall was due to difficulty in heating. Charlie's bedroom door opened off the living room and Molly's from the kitchen. The doors were left open most of the time to allow the heat to circulate. The bath between the two bedrooms had doors opening into each. Later a small room had been added in connection with her father's to accommodate a guest that came from time to time to help him with some phase of his work.

Adam looked around the room. It was large; desk, files, and bookshelves on one side, the bed, chest, and closets on the other. The room had been carpeted for extra warmth, but still had a fur rug by the bed, which Adam was glad to see was rather large. A round, potbellied stove sat in one corner of the room. He looked at it and grimaced, thinking about his centrally heated apartment in Anchorage.

"It keeps the room quite warm," Molly said rather stiffly. "You'll be glad it's here when it gets down to twenty-five degrees below zero."

She opened the door to show him the guest room. It was furnished with a single bed and chest. "We keep the door closed when it's not in use."

Opening the door to the bathroom she went in and closed the door going into her bedroom.

"The bathroom is modern except for running hot water. We carry the hot water from the reservoir in the kitchen range. This room stays warm enough if we leave the bedroom doors open part of the time." She led the way out, not offering to show him her room.

In the living room she went to stand before the fireplace. "Tim-Two, my father's employee and friend, lives in the cabin behind the house. He's lived here longer than I have and he'll stay. I'll pay his wages out of the allowance Herb will give me for living expenses."

Adam smiled at this show of independence.

"Very well. What does Tim-Two do around here to earn wages?"

"He keeps the stoves and the fireplace supplied with wood, and the reservoir full. He plants a garden in the summer and furnishes us with fresh meat and fish. I would trust him with my life and I intend to keep him here with me . . . always." She looked at him defiantly, as if daring him to challenge her authority where Tim-Two was concerned.

Adam, reading her mind more accurately than she realized, elevated that black brow again.

"You think you'll need protection from me?"

"Of course not," she denied hastily.

"Let me assure you that I have no intentions of raping you. I've never taken an unwilling woman to bed; not even a willing one that didn't know the score. Your virginity is safe with me until the time you wish to give it freely."

For one heart-stopping moment Molly stood there, her face scarlet. The violet eyes were bright with humiliation —but even as he watched, she bit her lips viciously and answered in the type of voice he had become used to hearing from her. Her rigid control, for the first time, began to intrigue him.

"I never, for one minute, considered myself in any danger from you, Mr. Reneau."

"In that case shall we consider the matter settled . . . Molly?" He said her name hesitantly and it sounded strange coming from his lips. "It'll seem rather strange if we keep up this formal mode of addressing each other after we are married."

She nodded.

The dark brows jerked upward in obvious mocking amusement and one hand came out, his fingers lifting her chin. He looked, laughingly, into her eyes.

"Say, 'yes Adam.' "

Molly looked into the dark eyes. They were friendly. The face was not quite so dark and forbidding, and the grim mouth tilted into a smile. Before she could help herself she said, "Yes, Adam."

He turned from her, putting his hands in his pockets, all business once more.

"We'll be married a week from today, spend some time with my dad, and come back here. I'll make the arrangements in town."

With that short pronouncement he went to the door and called Herb.

When the men left an hour later, the plans for the wedding had been made. Evelyn was staying the week with Molly, and Jim would come for them the day before the ceremony to give them time to do some shopping. Herb furnished Molly with an allowance check and assured her that he would take care of the legal documents. Molly insisted that a contract be drawn up between herself and Adam relieving him of any financial obligation to her. When Herb commenced to argue the legality of such a contract, Adam silently shook his head, and he let the matter drop.

The Robinsons had been sworn to secrecy. To all appearances, Molly and Adam had met a year ago and fell in love. The ceremony, which would have taken place at Christmas, had been moved ahead due to Charlie's death.

Everything had moved so quickly that Molly found herself too tired to think about all that had happened to her in the last few days. Her brain was crowded with a jumble of thoughts and impressions. Finally she concentrated on only one of the thoughts. She was not going to have to leave her home and for that she was thankful.

CHAPTER FOUR

A week later they were married in a small church in Anchorage. Adam insisted on the church service, saying his father would frown on a civil ceremony in a public building. There was no long white dress and no virginal white veil to trail Molly as she walked down the aisle toward the dark-browed man who was her father's choice for her husband. She wore a simple gray suit and a small matching hat and carried a single white rose that Evelyn thrust into her hand at the last moment. As she walked down the narrow aisle she noticed the church was decorated with vases of sweet-smelling flowers. She smiled as she recognized Evelyn's touch. This was her only act of unspoken rebellion against the unwanted marriage that had been forced upon her friend.

Molly was deeply grateful to her for her unquestioning cooperation and for the way she had strived to hide her deep misgivings.

The ceremony was short and simple and seemed like a dream to Molly. Firmly she had refused the minister's plans for having the church vocalist sing the traditional songs, which she felt would be meaningless for this occasion. Adam stood by the altar waiting for her as she walked toward him on the arm of Herb Belsile. She made her responses in a low voice, not daring to look at Adam, whose responses were strong and steady. When he slid the ring on her finger, her heart gave a sudden jolt at the contact of his firm fingers. She tried to draw her hand away, but he held it firmly and refused to let it go. He was still holding it when they walked out of the church.

Molly sat looking at the brand new wedding ring on her finger. A band of gold with diamonds encircling it. The beauty of it filled her with panic. This was the tie that bound her to Adam Reneau. She stole a side glance at him as he sat at the wheel of the big car, his face composed, concentrating on weaving in and out of the heavy traffic of Anchorage. He was so still, so withdrawn. Panic rose up in her, and she felt as if she were going to faint. She opened the window of the car and let the cool breeze hit her face, taking deep gulps of the air trying to alleviate the suffocating sensation that clutched her throat. With determined effort she pushed all unpleasant thoughts out of her mind. She would take one thing at a time. First, she must get through the reception and the meeting with Aunt Dora and her cousins. She would think of nothing else.

Adam said nothing on the short drive. As he turned the car into the hotel parking lot, he glanced at her and noticed her slight pallor.

"You're tired." His low voice was mixed with surprise and concern. "You're tired and frightened. Is it the reception or the meeting with my father that's bothering you?"

His nearness and the sudden unaccustomed tenderness in his soft voice was nearly her undoing. Her breath caught in her throat. She admitted to herself the knowledge that she had been fighting. She had felt a strange physical attraction for him. She closed her eyes. He must never suspect that she felt any warming toward him. That would be fatal.

"It's Aunt Dora and my cousins, Dee and Donna," she blurted out suddenly. She twisted the white rose she still held in her hands and refused to look at him.

"Dee and Donna Ballintine are your cousins?"

She nodded.

He raised her hand and looked at the ring on her finger. "Do you like the ring?"

Again she nodded her head.

"Are you never going to talk to your husband?" Gentle fingers brought her chin around and she looked into laughing dark eyes. She smiled back into them and started to shake her head. They both laughed.

"That's better." He still had a firm hold on her chin. "Let me worry about the Ballintine girls and Aunt Dora . . . okay?"

The dark eyes so close to hers were looking intently at her face; the golden hair, the creamy skin, the soft mouth. She felt a trembling in him where her shoulder rested against his chest. His fingers caressed her cheek and he said in a voice not quite so firm and controlled: "Do you think the groom could kiss the bride on her wedding day?" He touched her cheek coaxingly, and drew his finger to the corner of her mouth. It was a truly lovely mouth.

"You shouldn't . . . !" The breath was leaving her.

"I'm going to." He laughed softly and deeply.

He seemed to hesitate, then leaned nearer and laid his lips very gently against hers. It was a light kiss, but Molly's heart stopped for a moment and then raced ahead furiously. He released her and she looked into his dark eyes. They were no longer laughing.

It was in something of a daze that Molly got out of the car and walked with him across the parking lot toward the hotel. She wore only a light coat over her wedding suit and she shivered in the brisk late September wind that blew into Anchorage from the mountains. She was glad to leave the car, to get away from the destructive intimacy she had shared with her new husband. *Husband?* she thought desperately. *A man who was forced to marry me, who kissed me because he thought I wanted him to, and God help me, I did want him to. Husband . . . in name only, and I must not forget it. I won't forget it!*

44

It was a small reception, arranged by Adam, and catered by the hotel. A number of guests were standing by the buffet tables drinking champagne and talking. A toast was made to the bride and groom. Adam introduced her to some of his friends and she suffered through such remarks as, "Your bride is beautiful, Adam . . . where did you find such a lovely creature? . . . You sly dog, you, where've you been hiding her?" It went on and on. Herb, Jim, and Evelyn were the only people in the room Molly knew. Adam stayed by her side and after several gulps of champagne she began to feel a little light-headed and was glad for the supporting hand under her arm.

"Your aunt, Mrs. Ballintine, has arrived."

"Aunt Dora?" she said nervously.

Molly cast Adam a startled glance before looking toward the door and her aunt. Dora Ballintine drew her mink stole around her thin shoulders as she came across the room to greet her niece. A large, expensive hat sat atop her blue-tinted gray hair. Her ankle-length matching dress was flattering to her still girlish figure. Everything about Aunt Dora had to be perfect and it usually was. She swooped forward and kissed Molly on her cheek.

"Well, Molly! So you are married," she exclaimed so everyone in the room couldn't possibly help but hear her. "It must have been sudden. You didn't mention it at the service for poor Charlie."

"Hello, Aunt Dora," Molly said calmly. "I'd like you to meet Adam."

"I know Adam. I certainly do." She turned accusing eyes on him. "We didn't know you knew our little country relative, Adam. I must say, Donna was terribly . . . surprised."

"Was she, Mrs. Ballintine? I can't understand why." Adam said politely, black brows raised.

"You disappeared so suddenly, dear boy. Donna was

45

most upset—parties and things you were both invited to, you know."

"I'm sure a beautiful girl like Donna didn't lack for an escort, Mrs. Ballintine," he challenged coolly.

"Well, of course not," she said, turning back and looking Molly over from head to feet. "Why Molly, you look quite . . . pretty, but we are going to have to do something about your hair. I do wish I could have taken you to my hairdresser before the wedding. A good cut and styling would do wonders for you." Her voice was warm and kind, but to Molly's sensitive ears it was belittling.

Hurt pride lifted her chin. She opened her mouth and closed it again. She was no match for Aunt Dora.

For an instant a caustic look came over Adam's face, then it softened as his arm went around the slender girl beside him and he drew her close.

"I think my wife is enchanting," he said softly, smiling down at her. "This lovely hair will stay just as it is as long as I have anything to say about it."

Molly tilted her head to meet his gaze, her heart soared. How wonderful to have someone defend her, if only out of duty.

"I didn't mean . . . oh, here's Donna. Dee was unable to make it, but Donna canceled everything to come."

Aunt Dora's eyes brightened as she saw her daughter framed in the doorway, as if posed for a picture, waiting to catch every eye before she made her entrance. No doubt about it, she was beautiful. Tall, slim, vivid blue eyes, silver hair, and beautifully dressed. Crossing the room with a studied grace she came forward with hands outstretched; she had eyes only for Adam.

"Adam!" The soft husky voice breathed his name. "I couldn't imagine what had happened to you." Big blue eyes misty with emotion looked pleadingly at him.

"I've been busy, Donna. Busy getting married to your

46

cousin," Adam said evenly. "Are you going to congratulate me and my bride?"

The girl's lips tightened ever so slightly and she stood still for a moment and stared at him.

"Congratulations, Molly."

The blue eyes that turned on Molly told her that she was in love with Adam and she hated her with every fiber of her being. Molly glanced at Aunt Dora and was surprised to see her looking back at her with actual dislike on her face. *Wouldn't they be pleased if they knew the truth about this marriage,* Molly mused. *They'll never, never know, if I can possibly help it.*

A passionate protest was building inside her. It was impossible not to grasp the implications of the relationship between her cousin and her new husband. He looked so handsome, tall, and sophisticated. It was almost disheartening to see him and her lovely cousin standing side by side. They looked so right together; so worldly, so polished. She felt dowdy, small, and insignificant beside them. Donna leaned forward and kissed Adam on the lips.

"Darling, do excuse Mother and me," she said huskily and swirled away from them in a sea of chiffon, only a trace of her perfume lingering.

The meeting with Aunt Dora and Donna almost completely unnerved Molly and the next half hour was spent in an agony of self-consciousness. Someone handed her another glass of champagne which she drank too fast, and when they were ready to leave the reception, her head was really in a whirl.

"My father is anxious to meet his new daughter-in-law," Adam said as they were leaving. "We're staying with him for a few days before we go north to the cabin. Come and see us. But wait a few weeks!" They left amid laughter and good wishes.

"Lord have mercy!" Adam exclaimed as they made their way to the parked car. "I'm glad to get out of there."

Molly was grateful for the strong arm that hurried her along. He glanced at her only briefly as he slid under the wheel and eased the car into the stream of traffic.

She leaned her head back against the soft cushions of the seat and let her mind wander over the events of the day. Oh, to be back in the house by the lake! How much longer would she have to keep up this nerve-racking pretense? The reception was over, and she had one more obstacle to face before the blessed quiet of the country. She must meet Adam's father and convince him she was in love with his son. She owed Adam that after the way he stood by her through the meeting with Aunt Dora and Donna. Somehow she knew that her aunt and her cousin would never forgive her for marrying Adam. Their opinion wasn't important to her, but Adam's was. They would be spending a lot of time together this year and it was only sensible not to antagonize each other. She had learned a lot about the man she had married. *No wonder he didn't want to marry me,* she thought. *I'm not his type at all. It must have been a bitter pill for him to swallow to have to introduce me to his friends. When this year is over, we'll go our separate ways. I'll not depend on him too much—I'll stand on my own feet. It's the way it'll be from now on.*

Adam looked down at the girl beside him. *No confidence in herself,* he thought. *Fresh and beautiful, unaffected and untouched. God, how many men do I know that would like to get their hands on her? I'll have to be careful and not get involved. Family life isn't for me. At the end of the year I'm taking off as planned. I shouldn't have kissed her.* He didn't know why he did it except she is so . . . sweet . . .

"Shall we drive around a bit before we go to meet my father?"

She sat up straight in the seat and looked at him earnestly.

48

"I'll not let you down, Adam. I appreciate you standing by me when I met Aunt Dora."

With a twinkle in his dark eyes he said, "I see now that marrying me was the lesser of two evils."

"Believe it or not, I could have stood for Aunt Dora having control of my money, but I couldn't stand by and see my father's files destroyed," she said with spirit.

"Neither will happen now. We'll get through this year together and try not to get involved in each other's private life. When we break, a year from today, it will be as friends." He smiled at her. "Don't worry about Dad," he continued. "He's going to be in seventh heaven when he meets you. You're the answer to his prayers for me. Just be yourself and he'll love you. Try and make him believe you love me just a little and he'll be happy."

"I'll try." She smiled at him as if they were sharing some huge joke.

He drove into an underground parking area, angled the car into the area marked Reneau, and turned off the motor.

"My father lives on the top floor of this building," he said as they left the car. "He has a heart condition and never leaves the apartment. His sister, my Aunt Flo, lives with him. This has been a very exciting day for them, knowing I was getting married and bringing my wife to meet them."

"We'll be spending the night?"

"No. I've an apartment on the floor below. We'll stay there."

The color flooded her cheeks and she despised herself for being so self-conscious.

"You'll have to get used to being alone with me," he murmured consolingly.

She took a deep steadying breath. "I know."

Adam unlocked a door and they stepped into a private elevator. Pushing one of the two buttons, he said by way of explanation: "This elevator stops only on Dad's floor and mine."

The car slid smoothly to a halt and the door opened. A wave of apprehension passed over Molly. She looked up at Adam and he smiled reassuringly. They stepped out into a room that was surprisingly quaint and homey. A small birdlike figure hurried toward them. The lined face beneath the iron gray hair was wreathed in smiles. She looked as Molly always pictured a storybook grandmother would look. Even before she spoke the tension went out of Molly and she met her outstretched hands.

"Molly, my dear." She was obviously almost moved to tears.

Molly reacted instantly to the warm greeting from this gentle lady and kissed her on the cheek.

"Hello, Aunt Flo." Adam's amused voice was low and gentle. "Have you no greeting for me?"

"Oh, Adam, you bad boy! Why have you waited so long to bring her to us?" She reached up to kiss his cheek and he leaned down and gave her an affectionate hug.

"I told you she was worth waiting for, Aunt Flo. Now wasn't I right?"

"Yes, you were right for once, you rascal. But come, Robert is waiting and anxious to meet your bride." She led the way to a door at the end of the room and moved aside to allow them to enter.

"This is one of his better days, Adam. Take her in." She smiled at Molly and squeezed her hand.

Adam's father was in a rolling chair by the window. His penetrating gaze looked her over. How like Adam; the same dark, forbidding countenance and piercing black eyes. His hair was wispy and gray, and the lines in his face showed age and suffering. There was no evidence in his expression of the anxiety Aunt Flo had spoken about, but his frail hands worked nervously with the blanket that covered his knees. Adam urged her forward, slipping an arm around her shoulders.

"Father," he said in a low voice and there was an almost miraculous change in his expression as he looked down at the lined face. "This is Molly."

The silence that followed could be felt, tense and profound. Two large tears rolled down the old man's cheeks and fell on the blanket. His lips moved, but no sound came out. Suddenly he seemed to be very weary. The sight moved Molly deeply, her violet eyes went to Adam imploringly, then she dropped on her knees beside the chair.

"You're not pleased?" she asked with trembling lips, her eyes swimming with tears.

The old man raised a hand and drew her head down on his lap. His thin hand stroked the blond hair. Molly was vaguely aware that Adam had produced a handkerchief and wiped his father's eyes.

"Is it true, Adam," the shaky voice asked, "you and this girl are married?"

"Quite true, Father. Molly and I were married this afternoon." The positive voice had an effect on the old man. He gave the blond head a final pat and sighed deeply.

Molly raised her head.

"You have my blessing." The black eyes gazed into Molly's and she met them unflinchingly. "Give me your hand, daughter." She obeyed, feeling strangely close to this frail old man who was so like Adam.

"My son is a lucky man, but you are lucky too. Don't forget that. He is is the best of his mother and me." He looked fondly at Adam. "There is no finer man than my son."

Molly took the old man's hand and held it to her cheek. The depth of devotion between these two men was incredible, and it was wonderful to see. He had accepted her as a mate for his son. A feeling of complete tranquility settled over her. She sank down on the floor by his knee.

Adam pulled up a chair. Molly could tell that he was pleased with the way his father had warmed to her.

"Now tell me, Adam, how did this come about? How did you persuade this lovely child to marry you?" Molly noted, with satisfaction, the strength that came back in the old man's voice.

Adam told his father the story about the wedding being brought forward due to Charlie's death. Molly was fascinated at his expert handling of the affair. The most amazing thing was that he had not told his father a lie.

What followed was a very pleasant half hour. Molly smiled easily, her eyes going from one man to the other. They included her in their conversation and for the first time since her father's death she had a feeling of belonging. She had an odd premonition, that whatever difficulties lay ahead, she would be glad she had brought peace to this gentle old man who had so little time to live.

After awhile Adam excused himself, saying he would see if Molly's cases had been brought over from the hotel, but he would be back, because they were dining with his father and Aunt Flo. He took Molly's hand, pulled her to her feet, and folded her in his arms. Tenderly, he kissed the corner of her mouth. Molly felt a heady sensation coursing through her body. It was exhilarating, yet disturbing too. Unaware that her eyes were following him as he walked to the door, he left the room.

Molly looked down at Mr. Reneau who was watching her intently.

"You love him, girl?" he asked softly.

Without hesitation, Molly nodded her head. "Yes, I do, very much." Her lips trembled as the words came out.

"Ah . . . ," the old man sighed and settled back in his chair, his face serene.

They talked of many things. It was relaxing here in this room high above the busy street. She told him about the house in the bush and her dog named Dog. He laughed

52

with her about that. She told him of Tim-Two and the moose he hunted each year, of the jars of jam and jellies she canned, and promised on the next trip she would bring him a jar of each along with a loaf of homemade bread to spread them on.

He told her about Adam as a small boy. His determination to win each contest he was in, his stubbornness when he thought he was in the right, his deep desire to be accepted for himself alone and not for his money. He also told her of his grief following the death of his mother when he was a lad of twelve. The old man's eyes glowed when he talked of his son.

Molly felt a small nagging guilt at the deception of their marriage. She was glad she had told the old man she loved Adam. It had come out of her so suddenly and it seemed so right to say it. Adam would never know; she and the old man would share the secret.

The elderly man took his place at the head of the table that evening; Molly on his right, his son on the left. The delicious meal was served by the white-coated man called Ganson. It was obvious servant and master were equally fond of each other. Her eyes misted and the lump in her throat almost choked her when her new father-in-law invited the household help into the dining room to toast his "lovely new daughter." Adam was pleased, his dark eyes going from her to his father.

Later he whispered they should depart, because they would be expected to want to be alone. Molly took her leave of Aunt Flo then went to the old man's chair. Leaning down she placed her young cheek against the wrinkled one and whispered in his ear that she was pleased he had accepted her. He turned his head and placed a kiss on her smooth brow and squeezed her hand.

Feeling almost lighthearted Molly went with Adam to the elevator. Once inside he turned to her with serious concern on his face.

"Don't get too fond of him, Molly. It'll be tough losing two fathers in one year."

"No! Not so soon?"

"I'm afraid so. And, thank you," he said almost humbly. "You played your part well."

Molly was too emotionally shattered to answer.

They stepped out of the elevator into a carpeted hallway. Adam opened the door and waited for her to enter.

"Go in," he directed, his voice noticeably cooler now, as if trying to get back to the business relationship again.

She walked slowly into the room, her heels sinking into the soft carpet. The room was large, but lacked the homey atmosphere of his father's apartment. Comfortable couches and chairs were placed at random around the room and the walls as well as the various tables were decorated with objects he had collected on his trips abroad. Molly was impressed, in spite of herself, and smiled as she noted a priceless vase of Peking jade sitting alongside a hand-carved miniature canoe from his native state.

Adam grinned sheepishly.

"Not exactly *Better Homes and Gardens,* but it's home."

"It's interesting. I've never seen things like these." Molly looked curiously around the room.

"Go ahead and look," Adam said wearily. "But if you don't mind, I'll have a drink."

She wandered about the room looking at the different objects of his collection. The room was large and although it was filled with a profusion of paintings, porcelains, carvings, minutely patterned tapestries, and a richly colored Persian carpet before the fireplace, it didn't appear to be cluttered.

Presently Adam was beside her, a glass in his hand. She looked from the glass to his face, questioningly.

"It's very weak. You need it after today." He put the

54

drink in her hand, then with his hand in the small of her back urged her over to the couch.

"Sit down and enjoy it." He sank down in the chair opposite, stretched out his long legs, leaned his head back, and closed his eyes.

Molly watched him, her senses stirring in spite of herself. He was handsome; his dark features were more relaxed than she had ever seen them. Just looking at him lounging there, his shirt collar open, revealing the smooth brown skin of his throat rising up from the broad muscular chest, the muscles of his thighs firm against the material of his trousers, she felt a warm weakness flooding her system, and the desire to touch him made itself known to her.

She gave herself a mental shake and took a gulp of the drink in her hand. When she looked at him again, the black eyes were open and he was gazing at her. His eyes, narrowed and unreadable behind the heavy lashes, were staring into her violet ones, then dropped to her mouth, then to the rise and fall of her breasts. He sat up suddenly, his eyes darkened. He gulped the rest of his drink and got up to get another.

He returned to his chair.

"This is the first time we've been alone so we can talk." He ran his hand through dark hair in a gesture of resignation. "I meant what I said in the elevator, Molly. Dad won't be with us long."

"I couldn't help but like him. At first I was ashamed of the deception. It was like we were playing a cruel joke, but when I saw how happy he was, well . . . I was glad." She paused then asked anxiously, "If he has just a . . . short time, don't you think you should stay here near him?"

"That's one of the things I want to tell you. Dad knows about my research and how much it means to me. He thinks the reason I'm going north is so I can use some of your father's specialized equipment. He has devoted people to care for him here. They've been with him for years and I might add, it's a two-way street. He's devoted to them and looks out for their welfare." He whirled the drink around in his glass and smiled to himself. "My father is a very wealthy man. He pursued his interest, which was manufacturing a pipe that can be used in the polar region. It just happened that he made a lot of money at it. He understands that I'm interested in another field, and I'm lucky because his money makes it possible for me to do the things I want to do without financial pressures." He looked directly at Molly. "If I can be half the man my father is, I'll die happy."

"You love him very much."

"Yes, I do, and I wouldn't insult him by giving up my work and waiting around for him to die." His voice had become husky, and he raked his hand through his thick hair again. "I'll come back once a week to see him. I'll get someone to come stay with you, if it should become necessary to be away overnight. Occasionally you may want to come with me. Dad would enjoy that. But we must be very careful to comply with the terms of Charlie's will. I've the feeling that if your Aunt Dora could get her foot in the door, she would be happy to give us some trouble."

"I'm sure she would," Molly agreed, then asked, "Will Jim take us back?"

"We'll take my plane when we go up this time. I'll have boxes to take and I imagine you'll want to do some shopping."

"The only shopping I want to do is at a yarn shop."

"Knit, do you? Good, you can make me a sweater. Husbands should have top priority." His voice was teasing.

Molly warmed at his use of the word "husband" and teased back, "If I can find the time."

"If the weather gets too bad for the ski plane, I'll have the helicopter come up once a week. It can also come for us anytime Aunt Flo or Ganson thinks it necessary." He stood and stretched his long frame. "Are you tired?" He reached down to grasp her hand and pulled her to her feet. She had kicked off her shoes; he looked down in surprise. "You are a little thing," he said, touching the golden hair coiled on the top of her head. "You don't even come up to my chin."

"Yes, I'm rather short," she said, and added before she thought, "but good things come in small packages."

He threw back his head and laughed. It was the first time she had heard him laugh aloud and the sound was so pleasant that she laughed with him.

"Come on. I'll show you to your room." He led the way into a rather long hallway. "This is my room," he said as they passed the first door. "You use this next one. There are two more bedrooms; my friend, Pat, uses one and my housekeeper the other. She's away now, but when she's here, she helps Aunt Flo while I'm away. Oh, yes, Ganson will come down and fix breakfast for us in the morning. After that, you can do it if you want to. We've got a well-stocked pantry."

"I'd like that. I love to cook."

"I'm glad to hear it. It's going to be a long winter."

They walked into a white and gold bedroom with white carpet and white and gold French provincial furniture. It was beautiful.

"This room isn't used very often."

Molly went to the large bouquet of white roses on the dressing table. She bent her head to smell the sweet fragrance, then raised her violet eyes to Adam.

"Every bride needs a few flowers," he said.

"Thank you. They're beautiful."

"And so were you, Molly. No bride was ever prettier. Someday you'll have a real wedding and all the trappings that go with it." His smile crinkled the corners of his eyes and his lips. He turned to go. "Your cases are here.

There's a bath through that door. Get a good sleep and I'll see you in the morning."

He went out and closed the door. Molly remained still for a moment. A feeling of disbelief came over her. Here she was . . . married, and alone on her wedding night. *My husband treats me like a little sister,* she thought, *and it's just as well, for after all, he didn't want to marry me.*

She was more exhausted than she realized. She slid into the big bed between the silken sheets, but before she went to sleep, his words came back to her. "It's going to be a long winter." She sighed. It may be a long winter for him, but she had the feeling it would be all too short for her.

CHAPTER FIVE

Molly slept soundly that night. She had no dreams. When she awoke, she lay on her stomach with her eyes closed and listened for any sound coming from the apartment. After awhile she opened her eyes cautiously and looked at her watch. If she got up, now, she would have time for a bath before breakfast. She rolled over and sat up.

Her bare feet loved the feel of the soft carpet as she made her way to the bathroom. The bathtub was a marvel to her; big, square, it would take gallons of water to fill it. She smiled as she thought of the tub at home and the hot water she carried from the reservoir. She bathed, dressed quickly, and left the sanctuary of the bedroom.

In the hall she heard the unmistakable rattle of pots and pans. Cautiously she pushed open the swinging door. Ganson was at the stove and the delicious aroma of frying bacon reached her nostrils.

"Good morning, Mrs. Reneau."

"Mrs. Reneau? You're the first to call me that."

"Yes, ma'am, but that's your name, now."

She had expected to be tongue-tied and had worried about her shyness, hoping she would be able to overcome it enough to keep from making a fool of herself for the few days she was here. But it was easier to talk than she thought it would be. She climbed upon a stool near the table where Ganson was working.

"What do you call Adam?"

"Why, I call Adam, Adam." He grinned at her. "What else would I call that boy? I smacked his butt many times when he was a tadpole. Only one Mr. Reneau in this house and that's Robert."

He set two places at the kitchen table

"If you call Adam, Adam," Molly said, "you'll have to call me, Molly."

"Well, now, that makes sense, Molly. I'll do just that, but you better go get that lazy husband of yours before the eggs get cold."

Molly got off the stool. She didn't want to go to Adam's room and hesitated before going to the door. It swung open and Adam strolled in. Relief flooded her and the smile she greeted him with was warmer than usual. In cream cotton trousers that clung to his muscular legs and a dark blue shirt laced up the front with cream cords, he looked different from the man who stood with her before the minister yesterday. Her gaze was drawn like a magnet to his face.

"Are you showing her how I like my eggs, Ganson?" he asked with a devilish glitter in his eyes, dropping a light kiss on the top of Molly's head.

"Too late, they're ready." Ganson set two plates on the table and slid two slices of bread in the toaster. "I'll be back to clean up, or I'll send one of the girls down. You don't want me hanging around." He winked at Adam. "Coffee is ready, Molly." He left them.

"Molly . . . already! You must have made a hit with Ganson. He can be terribly formal unless he takes a liking to you."

"He's nice. Everyone here is. I was afraid I'd be shy and tongue-tied, but they're all so friendly I forget to be shy." She poured the coffee and placed the buttered toast on his plate.

"Almost everyone responds to a nice person. Ever think of that?"

"Yes," she said slowly, thinking of Aunt Dora and her cousins. "But it doesn't always apply," and added almost absently, "I liked your father very much."

"How about his son?"

"I'll have to think about that!" She was acutely conscious that his dark eyes were on her and her heart began to flutter erratically.

He grinned and Molly wished they could be friends. If she was congenial, if she could be a pleasant companion, he might not resent so much having to spend the year with her.

Adam told her he would be away part of the day. He explained he had arrangements to make due to his coming absence from the city.

"By the way," he said as if suddenly remembering, "I put some of my things in your room. Ganson would notice right away that we hadn't spent the night together and think it strange."

Molly could feel the color coming up into her cheeks, and poured coffee to cover her embarrassment.

Later in the morning when she entered the apartment above, Adam's father was waiting for her. They had a short time to visit before Ganson came to tell them lunch was ready.

"Shall I push your chair, Mr. Reneau?"

"What did you call Charlie, girl?" He asked rather gruffly.

"I called him . . . Dad."

"Then call me Papa," he said firmly.

She smiled down into a wrinkled face with gentle, almost pleading eyes. "Very well, Papa, but let's have lunch, I'm starved." She pushed his chair to the dining room.

Adam returned in the middle of the afternoon. Standing in the doorway of the sitting room, he watched Molly, his father, and Aunt Flo laughing together over an old picture album. His father was talking and suddenly Molly let out a peal of laughter. The old man could hardly keep his eyes from her young face and Adam felt a surge of gratitude. He came across to them and squatted down beside Molly. Her eyes sparkled; her high spirits had brought a flush to her cheeks. She had blossomed astonishingly in the last few days. To her surprise and his, he leaned over and kissed her on her still smiling lips.

"What tales are you telling my wife?" He spoke to his father while still looking at Molly. "It must have been funny."

"Oh, it was," Molly said quickly. "I'm surprised you managed to grow up."

"I wasn't all that bad."

"Papa told me some of the good things about you, too."

He adores her, Adam thought gratefully. *Bless you, Charlie!*

The days in Anchorage passed quickly and it was time to go. They went to Mr. Reneau's apartment to say good-bye. They found the old man sitting much as they had found him on Molly's first visit. He brightened noticeably when they came in.

"We'll be leaving soon, Dad." Adam reached down his hand and the frail hand rose up to meet it. "I'll be back a week from today. Molly will come with me later."

"I'll look forward to it, son." The old man turned his attention to Molly. "Bring her with you when you come. She's promised to bring me some raspberry jam." His eyes twinkled.

Molly bent to kiss his wrinkled cheek. "Wild horses couldn't keep me away," she whispered in his ear.

"Take care of her, Adam. You done good, boy. Real good." His eyes went from one to the other. "You two will have plenty of time up there in the north country to make me a grandson. See that you get the job done."

Molly's face turned scarlet and she dared not look at Adam, but she could hear him chuckle.

"You'd like that, wouldn't you?" Glancing at Molly's flushed face, he added, "You've made Molly blush."

A silence hung while the two men watched her with amusement.

"You're wicked. Both of you!" she sputtered.

"Listen to that, Dad. Accusations already." Adam held out his hand.

"Good-bye, Papa. We'll see you soon." Molly kissed the old man's cheek again and the last glimpse she had of him, he was still smiling.

It seemed strange to Molly to be sitting in the plane with Adam at the controls. He continued to surprise her with the various facets of his personality. By far the nicest thing she had discovered about him was the close friendship between him and his father. She stole a look at him. His lean and shapely hands on the controls of the plane were well cared for, but definitely masculine. His dark hair gleamed in the sunlight, his mouth firm, his chin obstinate. She knew the black eyes could be bitter or sparkle with amusement. He could change his face in an instant from a frown of disapproval to boyish handsomeness. He confused her, yet excited her. They had so little in common, and yet here they were married and on their way home, to her home. How had it happened?

"The trip shouldn't take over an hour," Adam was saying. As he spoke his eyes flicked her face and hair, framed by the fur collar of her coat. The wind had ruffled her hair and little wisps of it lay around her face. Her eyes were large and faintly apprehensive.

She looked down at the green landscape of forest and plains. This rugged, beautiful country was her country. She loved it passionately.

"It takes my breath away," she exclaimed, her eyes bright with excitement. "It's so beautiful . . ." She trembled suddenly, with an unbelievable happiness and impulsively said, "Don't hate it too much, Adam. The time will go quickly and you can take Dad's files, specimens, and anything else connected with your work away with you at the end of the year." Her voice held an apologetic note.

"I won't hate it," he said with an earnest frown. "I'll get a lot of work done this winter. Besides, if I back out now, my dad would skin me alive." Again she caught a side glimpse of the warm smile that altered his features so much. "I'd like to invite a friend and coworker out to stay for a few weeks, Molly. He's in Australia at the present time working on an expedition we plan to make. He'll be back soon and we'll work together on the new information we get from your father's files." He was looking straight ahead while he spoke. "It will make more work for you, so if you'd rather he didn't come, say so."

"I can cook for three as easily as for two," she replied quietly.

"You'll like Patrick. He's companionable, easygoing, but rather a wolf where women are concerned. I'll have to tell him the circumstances of our marriage. If you agree to have him stay with us, he can use the little room off my room. We can add a table to the one in the study so we'll both have a place to work."

It was apparent to Molly he had given this some thought. She glanced at him through her lowered lashes. He was looking straight ahead with calm indifference. The thought of a stranger living with them in the close confines of the small cabin wasn't pleasant, but she didn't know how she could refuse the request.

Adam landed the plane on the lake and taxied to the dock. Tim-Two was there waiting to catch the rope and lashed the plane securely. When it was safe for Molly to disembark, Adam held his arms up to lift her down. The warmth of his breath slid across her face as he set her on her feet. It was exciting to feel the strength of his hands on her waist, and she surrendered momentarily to the sensation of being held so close to him. It would be so easy to clasp her arms around his neck and hold him close. The thought surprised her. She gave a nervous little laugh.

"Thank you, sir."

Her life had changed so much in the past few weeks that it was hard for her to comprehend. She had been married, gained a new father, and come back to her home with a husband who thought of her as he might a younger sister, if he had one. She was determined to make it a pleasant year, one she could look back on with fond memories. One, Adam too, might fondly recall years from now.

Leaving the men to struggle with the crates and boxes, Molly ran up the path toward the house. Dog came bounding out to meet her. Knowing better than to jump on her, as his great weight would knock her down, he wiggled and twisted and his tail wagged as fast as he could make it go in his pleasure at seeing her. She fell down on her knees and hugged the shaggy head.

"Did you miss me, Dog?" She buried her face in the thick fur. Dog tried to lick her face, but she held him off, got to her feet, and the two of them raced to the house.

Before going to Anchorage for the wedding, Molly and Evelyn had removed all of Charlie's personal belongings from his bedroom and packed them in boxes which Tim-Two stored in the attic. Molly went to her father's room. All traces of Charlie were gone. The large pieces of furniture had been rearranged to give more work space. She was glad, now, that they had done this. It was no longer Charlie's room—it was Adam's. She went through the bath into her own bedroom, closing the door behind her. It was going to be strange having Adam in the house, sharing the intimacy of the bathroom.

She hurried out of her suit and quickly changed into jeans and shirt. She let her hair down, brushed it vigorously, and formed two thick braids that hung down over her breasts. Looking as young and fresh as a colt, she hurried to the kitchen to put away the supplies being brought from the plane.

Tim-Two brought in the grocery boxes and she busied herself arranging the supplies on the shelves. After many weary trips, all the crates were brought up as far as the porch. Adam came into the house wiping the perspiration from his face.

Molly was standing on tiptoes on a kitchen step stool reaching for a top shelf. He came to stand beside her.

"What are you trying to do? Break your neck?" He put his arm around her legs to steady her.

Molly hadn't heard him come in and was so startled she lost her balance and sat down on his shoulder, her hands grabbing frantically for his head for support.

"You scared me! Adam, put me down, I'm too heavy." Her squeals and laughter filled the room.

"Too heavy?" He twirled her around the room. "You're not as heavy as any one of those boxes I just lugged up from the plane."

"Please! Adam . . . please!"

He went from the kitchen to the living area with her still perched on his shoulder.

"I'll let you down if you find me a good cold beer," he bargained.

"Yes, yes, I will!"

He raised his hands to her waist and let her slide down the length of him until her feet touched the floor. Turning her around he took her two braids in his hands. Then, holding her captive, he looked down into her flushed, laughing face.

"Just thought I'd let you know who's boss," he teased.

Laughter bubbled as she looked at him. Adam, in this lighthearted mood, was a man to grab the heart right out of her. Pulses in her body were leaping at his warm, masculine closeness. Her hands were resting against his chest and she forced herself away from him.

"We'll just see about that." She danced away from him, trying desperately to keep him from knowing she was trembling from the contact with him.

The rest of the afternoon was spent unpacking boxes and putting things away. Adam worked in his room and Molly in the kitchen. Long before dinner time the gas-lamps were lit. The daylight hours were getting short this time of year. It was completely dark when they sat down to dinner. Molly had prepared a meal of homemade noodles and beef, biscuits, homemade jam, and cobbler made from canned peaches. Adam was hungry and ate heartily.

"Is there anything you especially like or dislike in the way of food, Adam? As long as I'm cooking it may as well be something you like."

The black brows raised and he thought for a moment.

"I like most things. In some parts of the world I've shut my eyes to eat the food." He met her probing eyes and grinned. "I especially like chocolate cake," he admitted.

They cleared away the dinner things together, then sat for a while before the fireplace. The autumn nights were cold. Adam stretched his arms above his head and yawned.

"I'm bushed. How about you?"

Across from him Molly yawned, too, and catching his glance, smiled apologetically. "Yawning is contagious."

"You're tired. Go to bed, Molly. I'll turn out the lights and bank the fire."

Molly went to the kitchen range, took the large teakettle of hot water to the bathroom, and poured it into the washbowl. Going back to the kitchen she refilled it with hot water from the reservoir and set it on the range.

"Hot water, if you want it, Adam," she said, indicating the kettle. "Good night."

"Good night," he answered absently.

Molly made sure all her personal garments were out of the bathroom before leaving it and closed the door behind

67

her when she returned to her bedroom. Turning out the lamp, she slipped under the covers of her bed. She lay for a while and was almost lulled to sleep when she heard Adam moving about. Presently she heard him carry the teakettle to the bathroom. *All very homey sounds,* she thought as she drifted off to sleep.

CHAPTER SIX

There is no lovelier place than the Alaskan wilderness in the autumn. The dark, drooping evergreens shadow the tranquil waters of the lakes. The beauty of the wilderness does much to inspire an even greater confidence in the people who live in the rugged country without all the customary trappings of modern living.

Soon the first snows of autumn would fall. Inside the spruce log cabin, set on the shores of the quiet lake, Molly felt, if not exactly happy, content. She and Adam had been living together in the cabin for almost a week. A pattern for their days had been formed. After breakfast he went to his room to work and she went about her usual household chores, always listening with half an ear to the citizen's band radio. Occasionally she would get a call from Jim going over in his plane or from a neighbor who just wanted to hear the sound of another human voice. Most of the calls were due to curiosity about her marriage and perfectly understandable to Molly. A wedding, a death, or a birth in the district was always news.

Every afternoon Adam spent a couple of hours out-of-doors. He was fascinated with Tim-Two's proficiency with an ax and practiced the use of the tool each day. The exercise was good and he thought it fun to see the chips fly. Some afternoons Molly would sit on a log and watch him. Occasionally she would take her fishing pole, sit on the dock, and tempt a fat fish to take the wiggling worm on the hook she dropped in the lake.

They always listened to the personal message program that came on the radio while they were having their noon meal. The people who lived in the sparsely populated wilderness received messages running the gauntlet from doctor's advice to shipping notices via this method. However, this meant the entire district knew about the medication Mrs. Jackson was taking, about the new snowmobile ordered by the Martins, and that the Petersons had a grocery order and the O'Roarks a guest coming up on the morning train. In case of an emergency concerning his father, Adam would hear the news during this time and Molly was always relieved when his name wasn't called.

The days slid by reasonably fast. Both Molly and Adam were involved in their own activities, their own thoughts. Adam kept the reservoir connected to the big cook stove filled with water and the evenings Molly took her bath he carried the steaming water to the tub for her. He was friendly, helpful, but not since the first day when he perched her on his shoulder had he been teasing or in any way familiar. He seemed to have settled down to the business of work, all serious and withdrawn.

He didn't ask her to accompany him on the first trip he made back to Anchorage. After breakfast one morning he merely announced he was going.

"I'd like to send a few things to your father," Molly said, "if you have time for me to pack a box."

"Sure. I have time, but hurry along. I don't want to be away but a few hours." He gave her a troubled glance. "You'll be all right here?" She nodded and reached for paper to wrap the small jars. "Keep the radio tuned in. I'd like to know you're in touch." She nodded again and wrapped a loaf of fresh bread in a cloth and tucked it into the box.

She looked rather apologetic. "I suppose this looks like

a trite offering to you, but I did promise him I would send it and I wouldn't want him to think I made the promise casually."

"Of course not. He'll enjoy it. I'll tell him you'll come with me next time." His voice was brisk and impersonal. He went out the door and down the path to the lake.

Presently Molly heard the sound of the motor as he taxied the plane out onto the lake, then the soft purr as the plane circled the house and headed south.

Alone in the house she decided it would be a good time to clean Adam's room. She changed the bedclothes, swept and dusted, being careful not to disturb anything on his desk or work table. She knew this was important from all the times she had cleaned while her father was alive. She did allow herself the luxury of looking in his closet at the neat row of clothes hanging there. Her hands lingered on the rough jacket he used for outside work, and impulsively she lifted the sleeve to her cheek and the smell of his maleness caused unfamiliar sensations.

An awareness of the absurdity of her action caused her to leave the room abruptly. A man of Adam's years and experience could never be interested in her. He had married her and he intended to make the best of the situation. That's all she meant to him. Molly hadn't the faintest notion of what the future held for her. She only knew that since she had met him she had lost the last vestiges of her girlhood.

The house was lonely without him. In just one short week he had become an important part of her life. She missed him. Angry at herself for daring to think foolish thoughts she threw herself into a frenzy of housecleaning. When the house was immaculate, she set loaves of bread to rise in the warming oven and on a sudden impulse stirred up a chocolate cake.

She tried to keep her thoughts from Adam, from what he was doing in Anchorage. Would he visit a woman

71

friend? Would he get in touch with her cousin, Donna, while he was there? She deliberately turned down the volume on the CB radio so she wouldn't be listening for the sound of his voice. In spite of all this, her ear was tuned to catch the first sound of his plane as it passed over the house.

Long before she expected him she freshened herself and put on a blue dress with a pencil slim skirt that made her look inches taller. Then she sat down on the couch to knit on the sweater she was making for one of Evelyn's boys. The rhythmic movement of her fingers was soothing to her nerves.

When the plane went over the house and began its descent to land on the lake, Molly's heart began to beat erratically, but she forced herself to remain seated. She was curled comfortably on the couch when she heard his steps on the porch. Their eyes met for a brief moment as he hesitated in the doorway and in that instant she was conscious of every detail about him. He looked big, masculine, and angry. It was difficult to comprehend what he was saying when he spoke to her.

"Why in the devil didn't you answer me when I called on the CB?" He walked over to the radio and saw the volume had been turned down. "What do you think went through my mind when ten miles out I couldn't raise you on this damn thing?" To her astonishment he was very angry. "One of the last things I told you was to keep the radio tuned." He came to stand in front of her with his black eyes blazing and his hands on his hips. Molly was too stunned to say anything. "Molly!" He practically shouted her name.

She sought about wildly for something to say. Then she lifted her head in sudden defiance, angry with him because he was treating her like a child. *Was that it? Was this the way it was going to be?* She would not stand for it! She was an adult and would be treated like one.

"You're pretty bossy all of a sudden, Adam. I don't have to account to you for everything I do. I can look after myself without any help from you." She sputtered recklessly because he was watching her with those hard black eyes and she didn't like the way he was doing it.

"Like hell!" he sneered. "I won't leave you here alone and have you deliberately disobey my instructions. I couldn't imagine what had happened to you or why you didn't answer. You answer every other Tom, Dick, and Harry that calls you." Her eyes were abnormally bright and his lips narrowed. "Well?" He said the word with sardonic emphasis.

"Why are you so angry?" Molly blurted. "Why am I, suddenly, so unreliable I can't be trusted to spend a few hours alone? I've spent many days and nights alone here with Dog and Tim-Two while my father was away."

Adam shook his head. "Listen to me, Molly—"

"You listen!" she flung, flushed and excited. "You think I've no brains at all! I'm an encumbrance to you! Something you have to put up with in order to take advantage of my father's work. Well, I'm sorry I've intruded into your life. I didn't want to, you know!" She knew she was being unreasonable, but couldn't help herself. Her eyes flared bitterly at him.

Adam reached out and with a cruel and painful grip on her forearms, jerked her to him.

"Now, you listen to me!" he grated between clinched teeth. "You've got to understand—"

Molly tried vainly to free herself. "I understand very well, mister," she exclaimed fiercely.

With a muffled curse, he pulled her up against him, his muscled strength holding her there, stilling her struggles. He pressed her head against his shirt. At close quarters his masculine strength had a hypnotic effect on her. She wanted to lean forward and let her whole weight rest on his chest. She felt a sense of unreality at what was happening.

His maleness made her legs feel weak. She melted against him. In the circle of his arms and hearing the heavy beat of his heart, she was conscious of a change in his breathing. It quickened.

He must have sensed her sudden, abject surrender. From somewhere far away she heard him say,

"Molly . . . Molly . . . ," the words sounded like a groan.

She felt his hand in her hair tugging her head back and before she could speak or move his mouth came down over hers in a hard, angry kiss that took her breath away. There was no gentleness, no tenderness. He kissed her savagely and thoroughly. She struggled and a little whimper came from the back of her throat. Then she arched against him, not yet understanding the strange new emotions that he had awakened in her body. She was only conscious of the pressure of his mouth and his long legs as his hands pulled the entire length of her body tight against his. Without knowing why, or what she was doing, her arms went up and around his neck and clung there.

Somewhere in the deep recesses of her mind she thought, *so this is how it feels?* This need, spreading through her loins, was making her incapable of feeling anything but this intense desire, and not understanding this sensation, she knew only that what she needed was him.

He pulled his mouth away from hers and looked down at her.

"Oh, Christ," he said in self-disgust. He looked at her lips beginning to swell from his kiss, and at her eyes wide and questioning. He hadn't meant to touch her, much less kiss her. He turned on his heel and went to his room, closing the door behind him with more force than was necessary.

Molly stood where he had left her. Her breath was still catching in her throat and her hands went up to touch her burning, flushed cheeks. She sank back down on the couch. She couldn't believe this had happened to her. The memory of the way she had clung to him brought waves of hot color to her cheeks and she wondered, unhappily, what he must have thought of her wanton behavior. She dreaded the moment when she must face him again.

The moment she dreaded came sooner than she expected. Adam came out of his room and stood looking down at her, his face considerably softer. Her body tensed and her heart beginning to beat erratically again as she withstood his dark gaze.

"I'm sorry I frightened you, Molly, but you did provoke me!" He took a small package from his pocket and tossed it into her lap. "A gift from Dad. He remembered he hadn't given you a wedding present."

Molly's troubled gaze went from him to the package in her lap and realizing he was waiting for her to open it, untied the wrappings with shaking fingers. Lifting the lid of a small jewelry box she saw, nestling on a bed of dark velvet, a pair of exquisite diamond earrings. She gave a small cry of surprise.

"I couldn't possibly accept these. They are far too valuable." She closed the lid on the box and thrust it toward him.

"Dad wants you to have them." He hesitated. "They were my mother's."

"Your mother's?" She flushed to her hairline.

"Yes," he answered brusquely.

She couldn't help herself. Her eyes were swimming with tears.

"Your father has paid me a great compliment and for his sake I'll be honored to wear your mother's earrings. But only for the year we're together. After that I'll insist you take them back."

"You're to keep them. They're not a loan."

"I couldn't do that, Adam, they should belong to your

permanent wife," she whispered huskily with a sinking feeling in the pit of her stomach.

"I'll probably not marry again and Dad gave them to you," he said stubbornly.

"I wish we didn't have this shadow of deceit hanging over us," she said softly. "Your father is too sweet to be deceived this way."

"It's rather late to think of that now," he said dryly. "In any case, what's done is done." Then, as his eyes mocked her, "Is that a chocolate cake on the table?"

"It's for you and Tim-Two. He likes cake, too, and any flavor will do."

Not knowing what else to do she took the earrings from the box and attemped to attach them to her ears. Adam watched her.

"Here let me do it." He reached down his hand to pull her to her feet.

She felt a tremor in her throat as his warm breath fell on her face. He fastened first one earring and then the other to her ears, before taking her by the forearms and holding her away from him. He tilted his head first one way and then the other as he gave her careful scrutiny. Her pulse was beating very fast. She was sure he had noticed, because he looked from her ears to her eyes, to the mouth he had so recently kissed, and to her throat where the pulse was beating.

"Very nice," he said smiling, "very, very nice." She smiled back at him, and he added softly, "Am I forgiven?"

Silently she nodded her head. "Then let's have dinner . . . hmm? I want to tie into that cake."

Molly caught him looking at her often during dinner. For the first time he helped her clear off the table when they were finished. Afterward he put records on the player and turned down the gaslight. When Molly went to sit in front of the fireplace, he went to his room, then returned with a pipe and a sack of tobacco before sinking down on the couch and filling the pipe. Using tongs he lifted a coal from the fire bed, held it to the tobacco, and sucked on the pipe. When he sat down again, he was puffing gently.

"You're full of surprises," Molly said and breathed in the good tobacco smell. "I didn't know you smoked."

He looked at the pipe in his hand. "I seldom do, but sometimes I like one after dinner, if you don't mind."

"I rather like it. Dad always smoked a pipe after supper."

The familiar scratching on the back door sent Molly to let Dog in. He followed her to her chair and laid his big head in her lap. She caressed the soft fur on top of his head and scratched his ears, all the time aware Adam was watching. Soon Dog returned to a far corner of the room, away from the heat of the fire. He sprawled in the corner, his neck stretched out, his heavy jowls flat on the floor.

"How long have you had him?" Adam asked.

"About four years. Jim brought him to me. He was just a bounding puppy then, all ears and feet."

"Is he the only dog you have here?"

"Yes. He's been a faithful friend," she said wistfully. "You know a dog responds to kindness, regardless if the person that gives it is rich or poor, skinny or fat, pretty or ugly, dumb or smart, I could go on and on . . ." she said with a laugh.

"Yes, that's true," Adam said, as the clock on the mantel sounded the hour. He got up to wind the clock. "Are you about ready to call it a day?" He was still facing the mantel.

Molly looked at the clock, it was half past ten! Embarrassment drew her to her feet. He wanted her to leave the room so he could go to his, but was too polite to say so! That was the reason for the small talk, biding his time until she went to bed. How stupid of her not to realize that. She went to the kitchen and turned down the lamp. Looking back she saw him rubbing his eyes and his temples. He showed no sign he knew she had left the room. Calling Dog to her, she put him out the back door.

"Do you have a headache, Adam?" she asked in a calm voice which gave away nothing of what she was feeling. "I can get an aspirin for you."

"I would appreciate it," he said, going back to the couch.

She took two tablets from the bottle on the shelf and drew a glass of water from the hand pump. She carried them to him and waited for him to drink.

"Thanks." He put the glass on the table, took her hand, and pulled her down beside him on the couch. She was so taken by surprise that she offered no protest, even when he put his arm around her and drew her close against him. She was terribly conscious of the hard muscles in his arm as he cuddled her, turning her so that her breasts were against the side of his chest and her head on his shoulder. He stretched his long legs out to the fire and leaned his head back.

"Each night when we sit here, I've wondered what it would feel like to hold you like this," he said tiredly.

She was stunned into silence. She felt his fingers at the nape of her neck and at the top of her head feeling for the pins as he pulled them out of her hair. Heavy, silken, and bright as gold it cascaded down over her shoulders. He brought a big handful forward over her breast.

"I've been wanting to do this, too," he said huskily, twisting a large rope of it around his hand.

Molly turned her face into his shoulder and nuzzled his warm flesh. The crackle of the fire and the ticking of the clock were the only sounds she heard above the beating of his heart. Her arm went around his waist and she held him, feeling the tension of the muscles in his long back.

He turned and buried his face in her neck, pushing back her hair and letting his free hand travel over her as if he were blind and trying to know her through his fingertips;

78

over her arms, down over her breast, lingering there, then to the narrow waist and on to her rounded hips where he molded her full length to his.

"Molly . . ." he whispered, "I don't know if I'll be able to keep my bargain not to touch you."

He raised his head to look at her. He was so close she could see every little detail of his face: the dark, smoldering eyes; the strong nose; the sensual curve of his mouth; the darkened cheekbones; the brown column of his throat. She could smell the warm smell of his body and the tobacco smell of his breath. She had never been in such an intimate position before and an aching stirred inside her.

She saw his mouth, the firm lips slightly parted, then it was against hers, rough and demanding with an insistence that sent her blood thundering through her ears. His hands were moving everywhere, touching her hungrily, fondling, an urgency in their movements. Naked desire mounted in her head leaving her trembling in his arms. She slid her fingers inside his shirt so she could touch his skin, some inner femininity giving her the knowledge of how to caress him.

Adam was breathing heavily. He tore his mouth from hers and his lips traveled over her face and then, as if compelled, back to her mouth. Unskilled as she was and although she clung to him with her hand on his bare chest feeling the trembling of his body, she sensed he was not getting satisfaction from her inexperienced lips. He drew back and kissed the violet eyes closed, smoothed the damp hair from her forehead, fondled the small ears, and gazed at her upturned face.

"Oh, Molly," he whispered, "I'm going to despise myself tomorrow. You're so sweet!" He kissed the corner of her trembling mouth.

"Tell me what to do," she breathed against his lips.

"No," he muttered and continued dragging his lips over her face.

79

"Tell me." She brought her hand up to his face and turned his lips toward hers.

His hands slid down her back and as if the feel of her shocked his senses, she felt his body shudder.

"I want you. I want to make love to you," he said, and then urgently, against her cheek, "open your mouth for me!" She parted her lips and his mouth covered hers.

The hungry demand of Adam's mouth was a whirlpool into which she thought she would drown. Now she knew why her earlier kisses had been so unfulfilling. His mouth was conveying his tortured need of her more powerfully than any words could say. He had aroused her and now she was no longer in control of her emotions. His hands stroked down her body with an eagerness he didn't try to disguise, which made her flame into receptive response.

He wanted her so much it was agony, but he knew so much better than she what this kind of lovemaking would lead to. A stab of remorse tore through him, and he pulled himself out of her arms and got to his feet.

"Molly, are you aware of what this is leading to? I want no regrets!" he said harshly. He took a long deep breath and looked at her as she lay where he had left her, her face hidden in the cushions of the couch.

A frightening awareness of the seriousness of what had happened came over her. She felt hot, shamed blushes covering her face and neck. Flushing with humiliation and self-disgust, she kept her face turned from him.

"Molly," he said softly. "You're young and beautiful. I'm alone here with you. I'm a man, Molly; a man with a man's desires. I've been used to having a woman and it's going to be a long winter."

The callous words struck Molly like a cold dash of water. "It's going to be a long winter"; he had used the words before. Tempestuous feelings were threatening to overpower her. *Love and hate,* she thought. She ran her tongue along the inside of her lower lip where his had been moments before. The cold fingers that had touched her heart on hearing his callous words had turned into a firebrand that was a burning anger.

Adam was still talking softly; whispering, persuading. "You've a lot to learn, my little innocent," he whispered, "but I guarantee it won't be against your will."

At that Molly raised her head. Her voice, when it came was shaking.

"Oh, damm you, damm you," she said with trembling lips, her eyes dry and blazing with fury. "It's going to be a long winter and you think you'll amuse yourself with a new experience, a stupid, foolish, willing virgin!" The words tumbled from her mouth. "And to think I was beginning to think you as wonderful as your father said you were. You're nothing but an opportunist. You married me to get my father's files and while you're about it, you'll sleep with his daughter because it's going to be a long winter. Let me tell you this Adam Reneau, I'm a stupid innocent, but I'm no man's plaything. If it's a whore you want—"

Adam grabbed her and shook her hard, his hands biting into her arms.

"Stop it! Don't use that word! You're my wife and what I suggested was for our mutual pleasure." His hard dark eyes were fastened onto her flushed, angry face.

"Your pleasure, not mine!" She glared at him, her face stiff with rebellion.

"Your pleasure too, Molly, I'd have seen to that." The irony of that ate into her. The anger had gone out of his voice and he tried to draw her close. "I'm not the kind of man to take a woman against her will."

Molly wrenched herself away from him. "I don't know what kind of man you are." She looked him in the eye, her mouth firm now with determination. "You're leaving in a year. You want no ties or emotional entanglements. You made that clear before we made the . . . agreement."

"You're right, I don't. I'm leaving at the end of the year. My plans have been made for a long time." His voice was level and controlled, but his dark eyes were bright with an emotion which she was not quite certain she recognized. "But that has nothing to do with now."

"Then there's no more to be said. Thank you for the valuable lesson I learned tonight." She flipped her hair back behind her ears and walked calmly from the room.

In spite of himself, Adam grinned.

When she closed the door on him, she leaned against it and wished she was far away, anywhere away from him. The thought of Aunt Dora's house was not as awesome as before, but this was her house and she would not leave it! Her frantic mind tried to think of ways to get him out of her house, out of her life. She could fake an illness and insist on staying in town. She could say she wanted to visit a friend in Portland. She could go back to the convent. She didn't want to do any of those things. What a fool she had been! The year to her now seemed endless. How could her father have been so wrong about a man's character?

She shut the door leading to the bathroom. With slow movements she undressed and slipped into her nightdress. She looked at her reflection in the mirror and pulled the tangled hair out from under the neck of her nightdress. Divided in the back it fell down the front of her, almost to her waist. She looked at it and hated it. In a sudden fit of rebellion at all that had happened to her, she grabbed the hand shears from her dressing table and began to cut. She cut off handfuls of hair and cried, her eyes so blinded with tears she could hardly see what she was doing. Doggedly, she sawed with the shears and threw the hair on the floor. When none was left to cover her breasts, she stopped, turned off her battery light, lay down in her bed, and buried her head in the pillow. Misery and humiliation flowed over her. She had acted like a recalcitrant child.

She slept fitfully during the first part of the night,

chased by nightmares, then in the small hours of the morning fell into a deep sleep to awaken with a pounding headache, a hangover of the emotional evening before.

She got out of bed, dressed herself in jeans and shirt, and kept her eyes averted from her dressing table mirror. After making her bed and picking up the strands of hair from the floor, she turned to look at the results of last night's ravages. She brushed the tangled hair that came now in uneven lengths to her shoulders. Her face was pale and her eyes were rimmed with deep, dark circles. Her mouth was slightly swollen as if it had been kissed many times, but it was set, now, in a grim line. She noticed, with a surge of humiliation, a small blue spot Adam's lips had made on her neck and drew up the collar of her shirt and buttoned it to hide the brand he had left on her.

Before her humiliation reached an intolerable level and she would be unable to face him, she picked up a ribbon, flung her hair back and gathered it in at the nape of her neck, and tied the ribbon around it.

A strange kind of calm had come over her by the time she was ready to leave the bedroom. She went into the kitchen as she did every morning. Tim-Two had already been there and the range was ready for breakfast. She put the granite coffeepot on to boil and set the table with one place setting. While placing the slices of bacon in the skillet she heard Adam's door open and turned to face him.

He stood in the doorway with his hands in his pockets with the same black thundercloud expression on his face that he had the first day they met. Under the slanting brows his eyes were blazing black between the narrowed lids. Not at all unnerved by his mood she looked straight at him.

"Good morning." She said it calmly. "You did wish to have breakfast?"

He lifted his shoulders and his frown deepened, if that was possible.

"Why did you do it?"

She turned back to the stove. "Why did I do what?" She was still calm and proud of it.

"You know what I'm talking about." His voice was louder. "Why did you cut your hair?"

"It's no business of yours what I do."

"It was a foolish, juvenile thing to do," he grated between clutched teeth.

Her silence showed her regard for his opinion. She set his breakfast on the table. The coffeepot was on a pad near at hand. Still not looking his way she lifted her parka from the peg by the door. After putting on the coat she took the remainder of the chocolate cake from the shelf and went out the back door toward Tim-Two's cabin.

The first snow will be coming any time now, she thought as she walked along the lakeshore. Tim-Two had been away from his cabin, and she had left the cake on his table. She and Dog walked the path toward the lake. The sky was a gray blanket and the dreariness of the day weighed on her. Tim-Two would be taking out the dock now that the lake would be freezing over. The crush of the ice would split the boards and break the posts. Always she had loved the coming of the winter. The evergreens would bow down under the heavy load. The whole world would be bright, clean, and shining. The small animals would scurry around leaving tracks in the snow. She would get out her cross country skis. She and Dog would take long hikes when the weather permitted.

How could she have been so wrong? she asked herself for the thousandth time. How could she have ever thought she might love him or that he was capable of love? He loved his father, but she didn't think he was capable of loving a woman, only using them. His father must have known that and that was why he was so pleased by their marriage. The thought came to her that Adam was a cruel man. You could tell by the cold way he had treated Donna at the reception. Not that she hadn't deserved it. Well, she was cured! It had come about the hard way, but she was cured. She would abide by her father's wishes, but at the end of the year she hoped she would never again set eyes on Adam Reneau.

Molly trudged back to the house. The cool wind had cleared her head. She made the firm resolve to take one day at a time until she was free of him.

The kitchen was empty when she came in. Adam was working in his room. She could hear his typewriter going. She shivered. It was colder and she would have to build a fire in the small potbellied stove in her bedroom.

Halfway through the morning she heard Jim Robinson's welcome voice come in on the radio.

"KGF 1452 calling KFK 1369. Come in Molly, darlin'. Big Bird is flying over and he'll set down on your lake if you have the coffeepot on."

She lifted the microphone and pressed the button. "That's a big ten four, Big Bird. I've got the fastest coffeepot in the North."

"Well get it perkin', pretty girl. I'll be there in a few." His voice came back and added because regulations demanded it, "KGF 1452 mobile clear and will soon be land bound."

Molly put fresh water and coffee in the pot and wished she hadn't taken all the chocolate cake to Tim-Two. She got out coconut bars she had baked several days ago, set out two cups and saucers, put on her parka, and went to the porch to wait for Jim.

Her eyes misted a little when she saw the familiar figure come swinging up the path, the usual friendly grin on his face. She ran down the steps and onto the path to meet him. His arm went across her shoulders and he enveloped her in a bear hug.

"I'm glad to see you." She fought back the tears.

"How's my Molly girl?"

"Oh, fine, fine," she said and the desire to cry left her.

They walked arm in arm up onto the porch and into the house. Jim hung his coat on a peg near the front door, while Molly was removing hers. He turned to look at her and the surprise showed on his face.

"You've cut your hair!"

"It's much easier to keep this way, Jim."

"Evelyn always envied your beautiful hair. She—"

"It's much easier to dry this way," she broke in. "Sorry I don't have your favorite cake. Will coconut bars do?"

"Is everything all right with you, Molly girl?" he asked quietly.

"Why wouldn't it be, Robinson?" Adam's voice came from the doorway of his room.

"Hello, Adam. How's the work going?"

"Fine." Adam came into the kitchen and got a third cup from the shelf. "I'll pour the coffee, Molly."

Molly sat across from Jim. Adam pulled his chair up to the end. The two men made small talk about the weather and compared the two floatplanes, now at anchor on the lake. Molly sat quietly, looking mostly at Jim, and entered the conversation only when necessary. Finally Jim rose to go.

"Anything you need, Molly?"

Before she could answer, Adam said, "Nothing, thanks, Robinson. I go to Anchorage each week and I get what we need."

"Well, anytime . . ." He spoke directly to Molly.

"There is something you can get for me, Jim. You know the lamp I use in my bedroom? Will you get a supply of batteries for it? The next time you go over, you can drop them."

"Sure, Molly. I know the ones you need."

"Charge them to my account at the hardware in Fairbanks, Jim. The one where Dad and I always trade." The stubborn, determined look on her face was disturbing to Jim.

"Sure thing," he said, putting his big fist beside her chin. "I'll have them for you in a day or two." He shrugged into his coat.

"Oh, Jim," Molly said, reluctant to let him go, "tell Evelyn I've almost finished the sweaters for the boys and I have yarn left for mittens if she'll send me the size."

"Will do, Molly. So long, Adam. Take care of my little sweetheart here."

Adam nodded.

Molly went to the porch and watched Jim go down the path. It was cold and she hadn't put on her coat, yet she dreaded going back into the house to face Adam. He was still sitting at the trestle table when she went in. She picked up the coat she had left on the chair and walked past him to hang it on the peg, then went to her room and closed the door.

She was standing beside her dressing table when the door crashed open. Adam stood there filling the doorway. His face was stiff with anger, his dark eyes spitting at her.

"Are you going to pout like a silly, sulky child all winter?"

"Get out of my room. I have a right to my privacy." Her nerves screamed, but her voice was cool and calm.

"You made me look a fool in front of Robinson." The words thumped at her like small blows.

"I didn't invite you to join us."

"That's what I mean! It was obvious to him and to me that I wasn't to be included." For a few seconds he stood glaring at her, breathing heavily, his nostrils curiously flared. "And . . . as for that," he nodded at the pile of cut hair on her dresser, "I should spank you!"

She looked unflinchingly back at him. "I entered into this arrangement with you against the advice of my friends and I have only myself to blame if I now have regrets. My only excuse is that I wanted to stay in my home. This is my home and you may share any part of it except my bedroom. I'll cook your meals, but I don't want your company. Do you understand?"

"And if I don't," he drawled insolently.

"If you don't, I'll call Jim and ask him to take me to Herb Belsile. I'll work in town. Tim-Two will take care of the place until I can come back home."

"You're stubborn and foolish enough to do just that! You would have your father's work destroyed," he said ironically.

"If it was that or my self-respect, Dad would want me to." Her voice shook as she said the last.

Tall and taunting, he continued to lean against the door, his grin mocking her as he sensed her agitation.

"Don't worry, little virgin," he jeered. "I won't seduce you! God . . . I can't believe you! You're twenty-five years old and know no more about life than a ten-year-old."

Their eyes met for moments. The calm violet ones and the mocking black ones. She turned her back on him and stood silently looking out her window. She didn't hear him leave, but she heard the door to his room close and knew he was gone.

CHAPTER SEVEN

Four nights later the first snow fell. By morning the ground was covered with a foot of the fluffy white stuff. Molly stood by the kitchen window watching Tim-Two come toward the house to stoke up the morning fires. She was up earlier than usual. Worn and disturbed, she had slept fitfully, waking repeatedly, her mind refusing to rest. She had been awake for some time before she dressed in her dark room, relieved that another day had come.

Tim-Two came into the kitchen after stamping the snow from his feet. Silent, as always, he checked the range, the stove in Molly's room, the big fireplace. Without a word to her he went out again.

She was sipping her second cup of coffee when she heard Adam's door open. This interrupted the quiet of the room so much that she looked at him in dismay. She had become so nervous and jumpy that she felt a sudden springing up of tears which she could not shed. His eyes were on the window and she sat quivering in relief because they were not on her.

"We must have a foot of snow," he said matter-of-factly.

"At least that," she answered.

"Are you not having breakfast?" He eyed the coffee cup in her hand.

"Not now. I'll have some later."

He took a mug from the shelf and poured his coffee. He

brought it to the table, sat opposite her, and looked at her pale face. The shadows beneath her eyes made them appear more violet than ever.

She averted her eyes and refused to look at him. She was not sulking or even unfriendly, rather utterly and deliberately indifferent to him. This was harder for him to bear than either rage or enduring anger.

"I'll make your breakfast," she said quietly, getting to her feet.

"Don't bother. I'll have some later, too."

She shrugged her shoulders. "I think I'll go out then."

"Wait and I'll go with you," he said, but she was heading for her room as if she hadn't heard.

Dressed in her warm parka and snow boots Molly walked through the snow. The air was fresh and invigorating, and she couldn't help but feel better just being out in it. Before she realized it she was walking the letters of her name, stamping out the letters as she used to do for Jim to see as he flew over. Laughing to herself as she jumped from one letter to another she failed to see Adam standing on the porch watching her. He came toward her and as she turned she saw him.

"Stop," she shouted, "you'll ruin my message to Jim."

"I want to help," he called back.

He jumped to a position under the letters Molly was stamping out and laughingly asked what message she was writing.

"Just my name," she told him.

"Okay," he said cheerfully. "I'll add my name to yours."

He started stamping out the word "AND" under Molly's name. She had finished the "Y" and stood watching him.

"I'll lift you over and you can start my name." Before he finished speaking he had reached for her and swung her

90

over. "You'll have to write my name backwards—you're on the wrong end."

He finished the word he was stamping out and jumped to the letters she was making, then on to start the next word. Molly watched him with somber eyes.

They had written "Molly and Adam," and he was adding the word "ARE."

Now he looked at her with a questioning smile. "Molly and Adam are . . . ?"

Molly felt the heaviness that had been in her heart for days suddenly lift.

"Are fine," she added. He smiled and jumped to make the final word.

The strain of the last few days was eased, if not completely, enough so they could be comfortable in each other's company. The next hour they walked in the snow stopping at the lake so Adam could check the plane before they turned toward the house. Dog spotted them and came out of the woods where he had been pestering small animals in their burrows. The three of them frolicked and played in the snow until Molly was flushed and out of breath.

The morning set a new tone to their relationship. The tension of the last few days had been broken and a tolerance toward each other was adopted. It was not the friendly companionship of the first week, but an acceptance of the fact they were living in close proximity in the house, and relaxed atmosphere was preferable to a tense one.

Molly was hungry when they came in out of the cold and set about making eggs and hotcakes. Adam sat at the table with the small transistor radio turned to the weather broadcast.

"How many pancakes?" she asked him.

"Do I have to commit myself now?" he answered with a grin. "I'm pretty hungry. Neither of us has enjoyed our meals for the last few days."

She nodded in acknowledgment, but didn't look at him.

"I think I should get the floatplane out of the lake today," he said later between mouthsful of hotcakes. "Sounds as if it's going to be colder and the lake will freeze any time."

"Maybe you should." She looked at him for the first time since they sat down. "The temperature can drop fast this time of year."

He stopped eating and looked at her intently. "Will you go with me, Molly?" he surprised her by asking.

"No . . . no." She shook her head.

He reached over and laid his hand on hers as it rested on the table and as badly as she wanted to jerk her hand away, to do so would be childish so she let him hold it. It was cold and trembling. His fingers were warm and firm.

"Can we talk about it, Molly?" he asked softly. His words fell into a pool of silence.

Any minute I'm going to cry, she thought, *and I'd rather die than have him see me. What is the matter with me anyway? Last night I knew I hated him and now I'm not so sure.*

"Things are never quite so bad if they're talked about," he persisted gently.

She raised her head and looked into the warm black eyes. She was surprised at the kindness and sympathy that she saw there and her heart settled peacefully as she felt his fingers increase the pressure on her hand. *He wants to make things right between us,* she thought. The relief that she felt showed itself in the small smile she exchanged with him.

"Okay." Rapidly her brain rehearsed what she wanted to say to him.

"First may I say that the last four days haven't been very pleasant ones for me and I'm sure not for you either."

Then he added with a grin, "If we can't be lovers, we can be friends, can't we?"

"I'd like to be friends." She looked him directly in the eye, which was her way when she was serious, and said firmly, "I won't be used, you know. It's insulting . . . humiliating."

"Molly, we're married! I meant no insult to you!" He said it earnestly. "I know you wanted me as much as I wanted you. It's nothing to be ashamed about."

The red flush that came up from her neck and flooded her face caused her to turn her face away until she could regain her composure. Her thoughts were so distasteful, she let an exclamation escape her.

"Don't look so distressed. It's a perfectly natural urge."

"But," she whispered, "I want to be loved before . . ."

"There are many different kinds of love, Molly." He searched her anguished face, his brows drawing together. "The true, deep love between a man and a woman can be very painful. Seldom do they love equally. My father was a slave to the love he had for my mother. He stood back and worshiped her from afar and when she died, a part of him died, too. I don't want that, Molly. I want to own my own soul."

"Is that why you were never going to marry?"

"That's part of it. The other part is that I want to be free to go when and where I please." Then taking her other hand he shook them gently. "What about you, Molly? What do you want?"

She gave a shaky laugh. "To keep from going to Aunt Dora!"

He grinned. "Molly, I swear that you'll never have to go to Aunt Dora." Still holding her hands he said seriously, "Let me say one more thing. You're sweet, beautiful, and charmingly innocent. Many men will desire you for these traits and the one you give yourself to will be a very lucky man."

"Thank you." She had never thought she would hear him say such things after their angry exchange of words.

"I'll take the plane into Anchorage and have the helicopter bring me back. After the lake freezes we can mount the skis on the plane."

"Will you see your father while you're there?"

"Yes, I'll see him. Sure you don't want to go?"

"Not this time. I think I'll wash my hair. I'll have the bathroom all to myself."

"You've got a spanking coming, my girl, for that haircut. Don't you forget it!" he told her sternly.

"It will grow. And it's a relief not having all that hair to dry each week." Her heart gave a frightened little leap at the thought of the threat.

His eyes traveled over her face and came to rest on the small blue spot on her throat. Her cheeks turned slowly pink and she looked away from the knowing glint in his eyes.

Suddenly he exploded in laughter and grabbed her hands to pull her to her feet.

"Molly, you're priceless!"

Her back stiffened and her chin went up in resentment of his ridicule.

"You adorable little kitten, don't get your back up." He gathered her into his arms in a big bear hug. He looked down at her, his black eyes full of devilry and his usually grim mouth tilted in a wide grin. Molly smiled reluctantly and put her finger over his lips.

"Kittens can scratch, you know." It was difficult to believe she was standing here this close to him.

He laughed again. Lowering his head he kissed her parted lips.

"I was going to spank you, but you're too big to spank. I'll kiss you instead!"

He looked down into her startled, resentful face and put both his hands on each side of her head. He shook it gently.

"You're a very kissable girl, Molly Reneau!" His black eyes danced with amusement. "I could learn to like your kisses too much!"

Molly laughed in spite of herself and turned to cross to the window. She looked out without really seeing the view. Her whole body yearned to go back to him, but her pride kept her voice light when she finally spoke. "Where will the helicopter set down when it brings you back?"

"I think the best place is over to the north. I'll bring my snowmobile back so we'll both have one. Do you like to ride?" He was getting out his big parka and heavy boots.

"Yes, I love to ride. Dad got all the equipment for me. We had great times on the snowmobile."

"And so will we!" he said firmly.

Molly felt immeasurably older as she stood by the window while Adam was preparing to leave. She welcomed the time she would be alone so she could sort out her jumbled feelings.

"Don't forget about the radio," he was saying, "and don't be attempting to lift those heavy logs. Tin-Two will be in. I'll tell him I'm leaving for a few hours. And another thing, leave the bedroom doors open so the heat can circulate and cook something good for my dinner. I'll be starving."

Molly turned, her eyes sparkling and her laughter ringing out. "Anything else, boss?" she asked in a little girl voice.

Coming close to her he looked down, an exaggerated stern look on his face.

"Yes, there is something else," he said softly. "Leave the volume up on that radio and don't you forget it!"

After he was gone Molly mulled over everything that was said between them from the first words that morning until he went out the door. He was a man of changing moods. So fierce and cruel when he was mad, but so sweet and gentle when he was pleased. She loved him. Her anger was the result of disappointment that he would want to take her to bed without any words of love or permanent commitment. She had to admit that he was honest with her. He was leaving at the end of the year. He could have had his pleasure of her and left her as he had planned. *We're married,* she thought, *but I don't feel married. Oh, God, what misery have I let myself in for?*

She spent more than two hours in a frenzy of cleaning. First the bedrooms, then on through the house until it was spotless. She had a dull throbbing headache by the time she was finished, and a splitting one when she had finished preparing a pot of stew for their dinner.

Although she didn't feel well she was determined to wash and dry her hair before Adam came back. She washed it in the bathroom and came back to the big fireplace with a towel to rub it dry. Her muscles were sore and her head throbbed viciously. Lord, how she ached! Her head felt thick and full. She rubbed her hand over her forehead and felt uneasy at the warmness of her skin. Wobbling a little in her pain, she went to the kitchen for aspirins, then came back to sink down on the couch. *I'll not be sick! I'll feel better if I lay down for a while,* she reasoned. She covered herself with the afghan from the back of the couch and drifted off to sleep only to waken shaking with chills.

She got to her feet, swaying dizzily. It was so cold! The temperature must have dropped. She managed to get two small logs on the fire before almost crawling back to the couch to fall into a deep, feverish sleep.

CHAPTER EIGHT

Molly opened her eyes and gazed into Adam's dark ones. "I didn't hear you call," her voice quavered.

He nodded his head, his black brows drawn together, as they were when he wore his grim face. Her eyes felt as though there were lead weights tied to the lids; to open them would take all the strength she possessed. Something deep in her mind told her he wasn't angry because she didn't answer the radio call. She drifted off to sleep again.

"Her fever is high," Adam said irritably to Tim-Two. "I'm getting a doctor out here."

Molly could hear his voice coming from a far distance. Loud and commanding, he talked on the radio, then in softer tones to Tim-Two; the doctor would come in the morning and for him to bring in more fuel for the stoves. She felt gentle hands lifting her. Two tablets had been placed in her mouth and she was commanded to drink by that soft, gentle voice she loved.

"I'll be all—right," she said weakly. Two weak tears started at the corner of her eyes. She shivered and unconsciously snuggled closer to him. "Please . . ."

"Please, what, Molly?"

"I'm so cold . . ."

A sudden feeling of comfort engulfed her as arms went around her and she was drawn close against him. The heat of his body burned into hers, enveloping her in delicious inertia. She heard him ask, in a queer, uneven tone, "Are you still cold?" She nodded weakly. *I'll be all right,* she thought, *if I can sleep for a minute.*

When she opened her feverish eyes again, she was in her own bed and a big man was sitting in the chair watching her. It seemed so odd to see a man in her room and before her eyes could focus she was gone again. She mumbled occasionally in her delirium and cried one time. Her father dried her tears. *Dad,* she sobbed, *where did you go?* Her hands were taken in his big ones.

"Sleep now," he said softly.

Several hours later she awoke and appeared to be more coherent. She looked at Adam sitting in the chair beside her bed.

"How sick am I?" she asked hoarsely.

"You've got a good case of flu," he smoothed her hair back from her face.

"You'll be cold sitting there, Adam. Are we having a blizzard?" She closed her eyes and drifted back to sleep.

When she awoke again, she was lying in a cocoon of warmth. She felt drowsy and far away, but safe and warm. She reached out to bring the warmth closer to her and snuggled against it. Arms held her tightly. She felt oddly at peace and didn't want to move out of this warm, hard nest. She lifted her head and looked at the man who held her. He bent his head, kissed her brow, and pulled her closer. The only sound Molly heard was the beat of his heart under her cheek, and his murmured words.

"Go to sleep."

She slept fitfully the next hour, then fell into a deep sleep dreaming she was in Adam's arms, kissing and being kissed in return. She awoke to find him sitting on the bed beside her.

"Hello," he said, "who are you?"

"I don't really know," she said drowsily. "Who are you?"

98

"I'm the man who held you in his arms last night. Remember?"

"I thought that was Adam."

He laughed softly and gazed down at her tenderly. "Feeling better?"

"My bones ache and my head throbs like a drum," she said weakly. She looked faintly puzzled; her memory returning in snatches. She realized she was in her nightdress. Embarrassment made weak tears come to her eyes.

"Don't think about it, love." Fingertips turned her head back and wiped away her tears.

She flushed under his gaze. "You didn't get much sleep last night," she said shakily.

"I slept fine. Don't you remember?"

"Yes, but—"

"No buts! The doctor will be here this morning. Go back to sleep. When I hear the plane, I'll have to take the snowmobile down to the clearing to pick him up. You won't be frightened if you wake up and I'm not here?"

She shook her head, her eyes already drooping. He sat there until she was asleep.

Molly slept off and on all that day. The doctor came and went, leaving medication for Adam to give her. He woke her regularly with the tablets and a glass of water, tenderly holding her up so she could drink. She heard Tim-Two come in and put fuel in her stove, and heard Adam talking in the kitchen. Adam cooked food on the range and from her room, she was able to hear him curse once in awhile as well as smell what he was cooking.

Late in the evening she awoke, aware she needed to use the bathroom. She lay dreading to make the move. Finally she could wait no longer and got out of bed on trembling limbs and stood for a while holding onto the end of the bed until her fuzzy head cleared. She staggered to the bathroom and closed the door louder than usual in her anxiety to hurry. She was making her way back to the door while holding onto the wash basin when Adam knocked, then opened the door.

"Are you all right, love?" He picked her up in his arms and hurried her back to bed. Lowering her gently, he tucked the covers around her. She was shivering uncontrollably, her teeth chattering.

He went to the kitchen and returned with a bundle that he thrust under the covers at her feet.

"Tim-Two and I have been heating stones on the range. I've wrapped them in a towel." Kneeling down he put his arms around her blanket-wrapped form and hugged her close, trying to warm her. Gradually her shaking ceased and he sat on the side of the bed.

"I'm making some broth. Tim-Two says you've got to drink it. He's been worried about you. He's keeping the house so warm he's about to roast me out!" he said teasingly.

"I don't know what I would have done without you," she said in a weak and trembling voice.

"It's about time for your medicine again and I must take your temperature. If it isn't down by morning, the doctor is coming back."

"No, Adam," she protested, "I'm better now. It must have been terribly expensive to bring the doctor out here."

"Expensive, be damned," he fumed. "I'll have him come five times a day if we need him."

Tears brightened her eyes. She quickly closed her lids so he would not see. He squeezed her hand, kissed her brow, and went back to the kitchen.

Later he brought a warm wet cloth and washed her face and hands. Then to her amazement he turned her gently so he could brush her hair. A feeling of sheer pleasure passed through her sore and aching body. When he had finished to his satisfaction, he put an extra pillow under her head.

"Now, you've got to eat something." He came back

minutes later with a tray he had already prepared, set it on her nightstand, and handed her a mug of warm broth.

"Can you hold this?" he asked. "If not, I can hold it for you."

She reached for the cup with shaky fingers. The broth was amazingly good. When she thought she had all she could hold, she extended the cup back to him, but he shook his head.

"All of it," he commanded, and she obeyed.

When he left again and she settled down in the bed, her confused mind wouldn't rest until she tried to analyze his unusual behavior toward her; his kindness and compassion, his willingness to minister to her. Could it be he felt sorry for her? *Oh, God,* she thought, *not that.* She didn't want his pity. *It's a brotherly feeling he has for me. That's it. I'm his little sister again and I don't want that either!*

She could hear him swearing in the kitchen. *He's all man,* she thought. Tim-Two came in the back door and Dog came padding into the bedroom. He laid his big head on the bed and little whimpers came from his throat. Molly reached out her hand and rubbed his head. Finally he stretched out on the floor and twitched his ears as if trying to understand why she was in bed this time of night.

Lulled to sleep by the murmur of voices and the warmth of the bed, Molly awakened when Adam came into the room carrying the transistor radio and the gaslamp. It was late. She thought she had only dozed.

"What time is it?"

"About midnight. I've been waiting to give you your medicine."

"I'm sorry you had to wait."

"Don't be. I've been listening to the radio. We've had a very big snowfall." He put his arm under her and lifted her shoulders so she could drink. "How do you feel?"

"Better, I think." Her voice was weak and she was shaking again. "But I get so cold."

"We'll remedy that." He took off his robe and flung it over the chair.

Molly's startled eyes took in the broad bare shoulders, the wide chest with dark hair going down to his pajama bottoms, the strong brown throat, and the muscled arms. He looked so different, so masculine, and . . . athletic. Her frightened eyes must have conveyed her feelings.

He laughed softly, turned out the gaslight, and lifted the cover as he slid into bed beside her.

"Don't be frightened, love. I can feel your heart pounding like a little rabbit caught in a trap."

He turned her so her back was toward him and wrapped himself around her spoon fashion, her head pillowed on his arm. He tucked the covers around them and enfolded her in his arms.

"Isn't this better than being alone?" he whispered in her ear. Then teasingly, "I'm not going to seduce you, kitten. I'll wait until you're spitting and scratching!"

It was difficult for Molly to think coherently. The nearness of the warm body pressing against hers with nothing between them but the thin material of her nightdress and his pajama pants was both comforting and disturbing. Questions lay like a coiled snake inside of her, the residue of past hurts. Then uncaring for anything but the moment, she relaxed against him conscious of the rhythmic thumping of his heart against her back.

His probing fingers smoothed the hair from around her ear. His lips nuzzled her neck. "Go to sleep. I'll wake you for your medicine."

Her hand moved to his and her fingers interlaced with his fingers. She knew no more, drifting deeply into her first natural sleep of several days.

She lay motionless, her body aching, but aware she was alone in the bed. She shifted her position and opened her mouth to call, but the words didn't come. Was she alone? Had she dreamed someone was with her? Weak tears ran down her cheeks. Then he appeared in the door, flashlight in one hand and a glass in the other. Relief flooded over her.

"Time for this stuff again," he said when he saw she was awake. "I've put more fuel on the fire, I think it's getting colder."

When he put out his light and got into bed beside her, he lay on his back and cuddled her against his side. Feeling the wetness of her cheek where it lay on his shoulder, he tilted her face and kissed her tearstained eyes.

"What's the matter? Head aching again?"

She said nothing, but stretched her arm across his bare chest and pressed closer to him.

"Want me to rub your back?"

"You don't need to."

"But I want to," he persisted, and rolled her so she lay almost on top of him. His hand went up and down her back, rubbing and massaging the sore muscles. It felt so good! Being so intimately close to him was wonderful. A small sigh escaped her. He chuckled softly and kissed her forehead.

"Having a husband isn't all bad, is it, love? Go to sleep. It'll be morning soon."

The next morning the ground was covered with deep new snow. The day began when Adam came into her room and sat down on the side of her bed. Laying his hand on her forehead, then his palm to her cheek, he pronounced her fever broken and said the doctor would not have to come back out after all.

Molly, a little fuzzy in the head from the fever and the medication Adam had given her the night before, lay motionless. She was too weak to do anything else.

"Hungry?"

She nodded.

"Good," he said. "You're going to have breakfast."

He was no sooner out the door than Molly reached for

the comb on her nightstand and flicked it through her hair, and then, making sure Adam was still in the kitchen, reached for the cold cream jar, and quickly dug her fingers into the cream and smeared it on her face. Seconds later she had wiped it off on a tissue that she concealed beneath her pillow.

Adam didn't knock at the door. He came into the room as if it was his own. He carried a small round tray with a bowl of something steaming on it. He put the tray on the nightstand and sat down on the bed again.

He smiled. It was a beautiful smile and it wrung Molly's heart.

"Good morning!" he said as if he hadn't seen her minutes before.

"Good morning." The intimacy of last night was making her self-conscious and she hesitated to meet his eyes.

He leaned forward and put his hands on either side of her pillow and, resting on them, looked down at her face. Quickly he bent forward and kissed her on the lips. It wasn't a loving kiss; it was a kiss, however, and Molly loved it. When he lifted his head, she wished he would do it again. Her dark-lashed violet eyes looked into his dark ones.

"You smell nice," he said thoughtfully. "It must be the cold cream." His eyes flicked over her face, taking in everything. "And you've combed your hair," he added.

Molly flushed and looked away from him. Even if he noticed, why did he have to mention it? He was smiling and the only thing she could do was to smile back.

"I've made oatmeal," he announced.

Once again he leaned forward and once again he kissed her . . . very gently.

He stood and placed the tray on her lap. "Eat," he commanded, and went out.

Molly didn't realize how much better she felt until after she had eaten. The meal had been simple, but delicious;

cooked oatmeal with a generous sprinkling of brown sugar, buttered toast, and hot cocoa. She wondered when Adam had learned to cook. She must remember to ask him. Moving the empty tray from her lap to the nearby chair she slid out of bed and looked around for her robe. Her eyes fell on the neatly folded clothes she had worn the day she became ill. An unexpected thrill passed through her at the thought of Adam undressing her. The nightdress he had chosen for her that night was flannel and revealed little, but nonetheless, he had seen all of her. A helpless feeling of discomfiture came over her. She found her robe and wrapped it tightly around her.

During that day and the days that followed Adam was kindness itself. He poured warm bath water for her and while she was bathing he changed her bed. He wrapped her in a blanket and laid her on the couch, tuned the radio for her, or fetched magazines. He cooked good meals and insisted she eat to gain her strength back. He never came back to her bed after she was up and around. At the end of the week Molly was well enough to take over her household chores and Adam went back to his work on her father's files in the bedroom.

CHAPTER NINE

After a week of below-zero weather Adam was sure the ice on the lake was sufficient to support the ski plane. He needed to bring in a large amount of supplies and it was much easier to get them to the house from the lake than from the clearing where the helicopter had to land.

He called for the helicopter to come for him after making sure Tim-Two would be around to check on Molly.

"You'll go my next trip. Dad is getting anxious to see you again. Pat will be coming out in a week or two so we'll be needing extra supplies. Make a list. It will give you something to do while I'm gone." He grinned at her. "And don't take a notion to clean the house from top to bottom. You're not strong enough yet."

"I won't," she assured him. "I've got my knitting. I'll sit by the fire like Mother Hubbard!"

He tugged at a strand of her hair, a crooked little grin on his face, and Molly felt her heart thudding. When they heard the plane overhead, he went out the door. She watched until he was out of sight beyond the timber.

Molly leaned her head back and gazed into the fire. She found herself obsessed with the memory of Adam's face—the narrowed dark eyes that carried such varied emotions when they looked at her. She had seen those eyes in so many different moods. They had laughed, teased, smiled, grown fierce with anger. She found she could not bear to think of them looking into hers with icy coolness in their depths. She wondered if she would be able to bear the loneliness when he went away for good. *It's lonely now, knowing he's coming back,* she told herself, *but how will it be when I know he'll never . . .* she shook herself. She didn't want to think about it.

Adam's voice came in on the radio, calling from the helicopter.

"How about it, Molly. Got a copy?"

She picked up the mike and pressed the button. Her heart was pounding.

"Ten-four, Adam," she said breathlessly. "I have a good copy."

"I'll be back in a few hours with the ski plane. Stay tuned in and I'll call as soon as I'm in range. Ten-four?"

"Ten-four, Adam. I'll be listening."

The day went rather fast. Molly had several calls on the radio from neighbors going over in their planes. She would chat easily with them until they were out of range. Tim-Two came in to check on the stoves. Later in the afternoon she became tired of knitting and made a chocolate cake. She decided to divide it this time and she iced one-half on two separate plates and sent a plate back with Tim-Two when he came again to check the stoves.

It was getting dusk when Adam's voice boomed into the quiet house.

"Break, break, Molly. Do you have a copy?" He repeated the call anxiously before she could pick up the mike.

"I'm here, Adam. How far out are you?"

"So you finally answered." He had a chill in his voice. Molly's heart sank, then lurched when he added, "I was getting worried." Her throat was so tight she could hardly answer.

"I just picked up your call. Do you have us in view?"

"I can see you down there." Then with a teasing note in his voice, "Is my dinner ready?"

"Now I hear the plane," Molly said. "And, no, I don't

have your dinner ready, I thought you were taking me out tonight." There was a faint giggle in her voice.

"I'll take you out all right. I'll take you out to the woodshed."

Then before she could answer he cleared off the channel.

Molly was happy. He was back again! He came into the house stamping fresh snow from his boots, his arms full of packages, his eyes sweeping the house as if he was glad to be back.

"Come, wife, and kiss me."

Molly's face reddened. She looked at his black eyes that were dancing merrily at her discomfort.

"Come," he repeated, and she went to him and placed warm lips on his cold ones for a brief instant.

"Hum . . ." he said. "I got a better kiss from Dog when he came to meet me."

Her eyes twinkled up at him. She took his packages and put them on the chair beside the door, so he could take off his coat.

"You're getting snow all over," she fussed to hide her happiness at having him home again.

"Did you miss me?" he persisted.

"Of course, it was nice and quiet all day!"

He hung up his coat, put away his boots, then in his stocking feet brought his bundles to the table. Opening one, he produced several bottles of liquor.

"If I'd had this the other night, I would have made you a hot toddy," he said. "And in way of a celebration, I've brought home some barbequed ribs!"

Molly wondered if he realized he had said, "brought home." Could a man like Adam ever consider this small cabin his home?

"I baked a chocolate cake!" she announced.

". . . and I brought you a present."

"You didn't . . . ?"

"I did."

He handed her the largest of his packages and stood with a grin on his face while she opened it.

Her hands were shaking and her fingers felt all thumbs, but she managed to tear away the paper and remove the lid from the box. She lifted out a soft, fluffy, violet-colored robe, and under the robe, were matching woolly slippers.

She looked up and met his eyes; her own were enormous in her flushed face. She couldn't move or speak.

"I knew it," he was saying. "I knew the minute I saw this robe it was the color of your eyes." He took it from her and held it open. "Try it on."

"Thank . . . you," Molly stammered. "I . . . don't know what to say."

"Well, just don't say: 'oh, Adam, you shouldn't!' " His voice was high and funny and she giggled.

"Well?" She turned so he could see her from all angles.

"Just fits," he said. "I knew it would. I told the girl you came up to here on me." He held his hand up to under his chin. "And I told her you were about this big around." He made a small circle with his hands.

She grinned broadly, her eyes bright, her face radiant.

"I love it," she told him.

It was a meal to remember. Adam heated the ribs in the hot oven and Molly made a salad. In the warm, cozy atmosphere of the kitchen they ate the ribs with their fingers before finishing off the cake. Afterward Adam helped with cleaning up, but told her he wasn't making a habit of doing so. Later, they sat before the fireplace and planned next week's trip to Anchorage.

"We should leave early," Adam said, "and spend about four hours there."

"How was your father?" Molly asked.

"Doing well, considering. He always asks about you."
He was sitting on the floor, his back to the couch. Dog had

come to him and placed his head on his thigh to be petted. Adam scratched his big ears.

Molly bowed her head over the sweater she had started for Adam. She had bought the Australian wool last year on an impulse, not really knowing what she was going to make out of it. Just this afternoon it had occurred to her that the off-white color would go well with Adam's dark good looks. She hadn't told him what she was working on and he hadn't asked.

Now that the weather had turned cold all the doors inside the cabin were left open because they needed the extra heat in the bedrooms. The bathroom doors were left open at night when the room wasn't in use. Adam, being the last each night to use the room, opened both the door to Molly's room and his own before he went to bed.

Molly, now, lay in her bed and listened to the sounds coming from the other bedroom. She thought of the two nights he had spent in her bed. How sweet and gentle he had been! *Would it be so wrong,* she thought, *to let him make love to me? We're married! Could I bear for him to leave me after knowing what it feels like to be possessed by him?*

She lay on her back, eyes closed, remembering how he had rubbed her back, caressed her, and folded her in his arms to keep her warm. She could feel the stubble on his chin that morning as he slept with it resting against her forehead. Her heart began to beat rapidly and a hunger for him like a pain went through her; through her lips, her breasts, and into her loins. The pain grew and the blood rushed to her face. Disgusted at her thoughts she flopped over on her stomach and buried her head in the pillow. *What's the matter with me?* she thought. *I'm like a bitch in heat.* Of one thing she was almost sure: Adam would keep their relationship on the present level. If it should ever change, she would have to be the one to make the first move.

Molly kept herself busy during the days that followed. The weather was cold, always hovering around the zero mark. She spent an hour each day out of the house. Tim-Two brought out the sled and harness. She hitched up Dog, who loved every minute of pulling the sled. They went with Tim-Two on short runs to his trap lines. This wasn't Molly's favorite thing to do, and she was always relieved when they found them empty.

The moose were coming down out of the hills and into the timber now. Soon the hunting season would be here and Tim-Two would shoot one for the meat it would supply. Molly never stayed around to watch the slaughter or the butchering of the meat. When Tim-Two brought in the neatly wrapped packages from the woodshed, where they were frozen, she would pretend they had come from the meat market in town.

One afternoon she took the snowmobile out alone and enjoyed a ride down the path to the lake and through the timber to the clearing where the helicopter landed. Believing that she had been gone only an hour she was surprised when she returned to find Adam preparing to go look for her.

"Where in the hell have you been?" he demanded, with the thundercloud look on his face.

"Only down through . . . the timber," she stammered, surprised at his anger. "Why?"

"Why?" he repeated. "You've been gone an hour, that's why!"

She couldn't understand why he was so angry, and the questioning look in her violet eyes told him she didn't understand.

"I saw fresh wolf tracks around the lake yesterday. You're not to go out of sight of this house without me or Tim-Two. Is that understood?"

"This is the first time I've been out by myself." Her eyes looked squarely into his.

"And it will be the last time, my girl!" he said firmly. "Tim-Two thinks there's a wolverine about. He saw the sign in his trap lines."

"But—" she started to explain she had lived here for five years and wasn't exactly a greenhorn, but he wouldn't let her say it.

"Don't argue, Molly. I've told you what you cannot do and that's the end of it." He took off his parka. As far as he was concerned the matter was closed.

At first Molly was angry at his high-handed method of telling her about the danger, but after thinking about it she understood his concern. Although it was early winter and there was still plenty of small game for the wolves, they were a dangerous lot and not to be trusted. The unpredictable wolverine was another matter altogether. They attacked when and where they wanted, if they were hungry or not, just for the sheer pleasure of the kill. Molly had seen the results of a wolverine kill and it was not a pleasant sight.

The next day Molly hitched Dog to the sled for a ride around the yard. Adam came out to go with her and they headed for the frozen lake. She rode on the sled and Adam on the runners behind. Dog was in rare form. He had two playmates and for more than an hour they played like two children on the ice. When they came back to the house, they sat before the fire and drank hot cocoa. It felt as though they'd been together forever, there was such ease and companionship between them.

The day before the trip to Anchorage Adam asked if there was any reason why they couldn't stay overnight in the apartment. He would like to stay two nights, he said, as he had some business he should attend to. They were eating their evening meal at the trestle table and Molly looked across at him in her questioning way.

"It's perfectly legal as far as the will is concerned, Molly. Charlie didn't mean for us to spend every day here.

And I'm sure your aunt would think twice before she tackled me and my father."

"I wasn't thinking of that," she said. "I was thinking I wouldn't go this time and you could take care of your business. I'll go with you when you go again for the day."

"No, for two reasons. First and foremost, I'll not leave you here alone overnight, and second, I promised Dad I'd bring you the next time I came in."

"Then it's settled," she conceded.

"I'll take you out to dinner," he promised. "We'll do a night on the town."

"No," she said quickly, "that won't be necessary. I'm not taking suitable evening clothes." Not that she had suitable clothes to take, she thought dryly.

"That's no problem. We'll buy something."

"No . . . no, I'd rather not."

"Is that all you can say—'no, no!' " He laughed at her. "Well, we'll see." He was in one of his teasing moods and Molly couldn't help but laugh with him.

That night she looked over her simple wardrobe. She didn't have much to choose from. Finally, she picked out two simple dresses to wear during the day, and a pair of wool slacks with matching sweater to wear to and from the city. She laid out toilet articles, a nightie, and the robe and slippers Adam had given her. As an afterthought she tucked in the diamond earrings, the gift from his father.

CHAPTER TEN

They walked down the snow-packed path to the plane. Adam tucked her in the seat and wrapped her with a blanket before fastening her seat belt. She never tired of watching him. He was so confident, so capable. She had dreaded the trip to town, but now that she was actually on her way, she felt a little thrill of excitement and looked forward to seeing Adam's father and his Aunt Flo again. The one thing she was sure of was a welcome there. She felt none of the apprehension of the first visit.

Once the plane was in the air Adam told her something about Anchorage. She and her father did all their business in Fairbanks and she admitted she knew little about Alaska's largest city. Nearly every second Alaskan lives in Anchorage, he told her. It was a sprawling modern city of almost two hundred thousand, located between Cook Inlet and the Chugach mountains. There was considerable damage done to the city during the 1964 earthquake, but the rebuilding had been completed, and the city had become a headquarters for large corporations and government agencies. Adam's father's company was headquartered there. He said he had little to do with the company, but owned voting stock and attended board meetings.

Adam expressed regret that his native state was fast becoming a "get-rich-quick" oil boom state. Being a strict conservationist, he'd rather the state stayed poor and they kept what they had. He was "between the devil and the

114

deep blue sea," he explained, wanting to keep Alaska as it was and owning stock in a company manufacturing pipe to lay it to waste.

Adam set the plane down on a runway set aside for the landing of ski planes and they were towed into the hangar by a small vehicle. Adam's car was in a nearby garage and they were soon on the way to his apartment building. They passed the famous Captain Cook Hotel, and he teasingly told her if she was a "good" girl, he would take her there for dinner.

Molly said nothing, but the thought of going out with him brought terror to her heart. Her confidence was fast leaving her. In the city he appeared different from what he was with her in the cabin. She was frightened that she would do something ridiculous and embarrass him.

As they were going up in the elevator of the apartment building Adam suggested they stop at his apartment and freshen up before going up to see his father. He opened the door and Molly went in and looked around. She was not as astonished at his collection of things as she had been the first time she visited here. Somehow after knowing him better she understood his desire to keep these pleasant mementos of his travels.

He carried her case to the bedroom she had used before.

"Shall we have a good bath and use all the hot water we want to?" Amusement brightened his dark eyes.

"Why, not," she answered. "What time does your father expect us?"

"I'll call and tell Ganson we'll be up in about an hour. Okay?"

"Okay," she echoed. "Are you glad to be back in civilization?"

"I don't know if you would call this civilization. It's pretty much of a jungle, but I'll admit I enjoy the hot shower!"

Molly hung her two dresses and the robe in the closet,

115

and opened the drawer of the dressing table to put away her toilet articles. A lipstick rolled to the front of the drawer when she opened it. She picked it up and looked at it. It wasn't one of hers and she was sure it hadn't been in the drawer when she was here before. A queer, tight little feeling closed in around her heart. Had Adam brought a girl here on one of his visits to see his father? He said he was accustomed to being with a woman. No! She wouldn't think about it! She had no right to feel disappointed. He was perfectly free to do as he pleased as long as he abided by the terms of her father's will. She put the offending tube out of her sight in another drawer and went into the bathroom to take her bath.

Wallowing in the deep tub filled with the sweet-scented water, Molly forced her mind to dwell on how she could dress her hair. Not being used to the shorter length, she had been letting it hang, held back by a band, but that wouldn't do here. She didn't want to look like a teen-ager. She decided to try and roll it into a flat bun on top of her head, somewhat as she used to coil her braids. If that wouldn't do, she would try a bun at the nape of her neck. Either way would make her look a little more sophisticated.

She chose to wear the plum-colored wool dress. It had simple lines and a flared skirt that swayed gently as she walked. She slipped her feet into the black pumps and sat for a long while brushing her hair, trying to decide on a style. After several attempts to make a bun on top of her head she had to settle for one at the nape of her neck. She was applying plum-colored lipstick to match her dress when Adam knocked on the door, then opened it and came in. She looked at him through the dressing table mirror. A lump rose up in her throat so that she could hardly swallow.

He had just come from his shower. His hair was damp

and curling. He had on a light tan knit shirt tucked snugly into navy blue trousers. The long-sleeve shirt was opened at the neck and she caught a glimpse of the curly black hair on his chest where she had once laid her cheek. His eyes held hers for a long moment. The pulse at the base of her throat beat madly, and she saw him lower his eyes to look at it. She remembered the spot his mouth had made on her neck and she desperately wanted to look to see if it was still there, but she didn't dare take her eyes from his. He broke the silence.

"Why did you pin up your hair for God's sake?" He came to where she sat facing the mirror. "What's the matter with the way you wear it at home?"

"Because this makes me look my age," she replied, her voice quite matter-of-fact.

"It makes you look ridiculous!" His fingers went to her neck and he started to remove the pins.

"Adam!" She tried to twist away from him. "It took me a long time to get it pinned up."

"I like it the other way," he insisted. "Beautiful things should not be pinned up or tied down." He continued taking out the pins. "Now give me the brush." He held out his hand.

She slapped the brush down into his hand with emphasis. He stood behind her and brushed her hair with long, even strokes. He brushed it straight back over her forehead and behind her ears. He brushed it from under the nape of her neck. At last he was satisfied and handed the brush back to her.

"Where's one of those ribbon things?"

"I didn't bring one," she said sulkily.

"I'll send Ganson to get one."

"No . . . no . . . , I've got a white one here in the drawer."

"I thought you did," he grinned. "I saw it this morning."

117

She handed it to him and he slipped it under her hair and across the top of her head.

"Now you look like Molly again." He took her hand and pulled her up from the seat. "You look very, very pretty!" he said, and kissed her on the nose. "Let's go. Dad is waiting for us."

Molly received the same welcome as the first time she came to the apartment. Adam's Aunt Flo met her in the hall as soon as the elevator door opened and came forward with open arms. She embraced her enthusiastically, then held her away and looked at her.

"Such beautiful golden hair, such lovely skin and innocent eyes. Adam, I was afraid I had dreamed her," she exclaimed.

"She's real all right, Aunt Flo." He looked down proudly as his aunt turned her toward the sitting room. He caught Molly's eye and lifted his eyebrows with questionable humor. A feeling of guilt flooded over her. The deceit they were practicing was abhorrent to her. This dear little lady was so ready and willing to accept her. Molly knew she could grow to love her as well as Adam's father.

They entered the sitting room and found the old man in a chair by the fireplace. His eyes were on the door as they came through it, and as they came forward he had eyes only for Molly. To her he looked much the same as he did the last time they were there and she went to him immediately, genuinely glad to see him again. She forgot Adam and the part she was supposed to play. She took his frail hand and bent to kiss his wrinkled cheek.

"Hello, Papa," she said softly. She was surprised at the strength of the hand that held hers.

"Hello, daughter," the weak voice replied. "I was beginning to think you weren't coming back to see me."

"Oh, yes, I was coming," she said archly, "but I had a bout with the flu and didn't want to bring you my bugs."

He chuckled and looked at Adam. "Hello, son." The

dimmed eyes which took in the tall, dark-haired figure that bent over him were filled with love and admiration.

"How are you, Dad?" Adam's face held the look Molly had seen before when he greeted his father.

She looked from father to son and felt a warm glow as if she were witness to a rare and wonderful thing. The love and admiration they each had for each other were obvious. *There must be some fifty-odd years between their ages,* she thought, *but there is no generation gap here.*

"Sit down, sit down," the old man was saying.

Adam pulled a footstool up close to his father's chair for Molly because the old man had not released her hand. He sat opposite them and stretched out his long legs. Molly flushed when she met his eyes and looked away. She wished he would leave. She sincerely liked his father and didn't want him thinking she was play-acting. He settled himself to stay so she decided she would have to try and forget he was there.

"So you're going to stay two nights." The father was addressing the son.

"We'll be staying tonight and tomorrow night. Tomorrow night I'm taking Molly out on the town."

Oh, no, not that again, she thought. She didn't dare look at him lest he see the fright in her eyes.

"Good, good." Mr. Reneau looked at Molly affectionately. "Adam told me you had cut your hair, daughter. I was a little disappointed until he explained how hard it was to take care of, up there in the woods. Now, I think I like it. You're young and there's plenty of time for you to do it up like an old woman!" This was quite a long speech for the old man.

Molly gave an exasperated sigh. It was irritating to know they had discussed something as personal as her hair. At least Adam hadn't told him she cut it in a fit of temper.

119

"Thank you for the earrings, Papa," she said. "I would have worn them tonight, but I didn't think diamond earrings were appropriate with a street dress." She smiled at him mischievously.

"Adam's mother was young like you when I gave them to her. She wore them almost every day." His face creased even more in a gentle smile.

Molly talked on and on. The old man hardly took his eyes from her face. She told him about the snow and the fun they had hitching Dog to the sled, about going to check Tim-Two's trap lines, and the moose hunt in another week or so. She explained that they only took one moose a season and that was for the supply of meat. She also told him that she couldn't stand to watch the butchering because if she did, she couldn't eat a bite of the meat. He smiled and nodded his head and told her Adam's mother was like that. She told him about the wolf tracks Adam found down by the lake. Glancing at Adam she saw the amusement in his eyes and she turned her face stubbornly, and refused to look at him. She was sure she heard him chuckle and almost turned to glare at him. Just in time she controlled the desire and went on to tell about the wolverine sign Tim-Two had found, and also how fast their wood supply was going down due to the cold.

Adam sat quietly, never uttering a word. Molly was embarrassed that she had talked so much. He was lazing back in his chair, his eyes between the dark lashes were mere slits, but he had an impish grin on his face.

"Adam," she said, exasperated at his silence. "Aren't you going to say anything?"

"I couldn't get a word in if I wanted to. Your mouth has been going ninety miles an hour." That devilish look was in his eyes again, the one that was always there when he knew he was getting under her skin.

"Don't mind him. You should be used to his teasing

way, by now." Mr. Reneau gently shook the hand that was still in his.

"I could . . . hit him, when he gets in that devilish mood," she said heatedly.

The old man laughed so hard Molly was afraid for him. He laughed until the tears came. She looked at Adam; he was laughing too, so she guessed there was no danger to the old man.

"Good for you," Mr. Reneau said finally. "Why don't you try it sometime?"

"I just might do that!" Molly said with spirit.

"If you're going to be here with my dad, I'll make some phone calls." Adam went to the door still grinning.

"I'll be here," she said, ignoring his retreating back.

There was little sleep for Molly that night. All through the long dark hours she tossed restlessly. In spite of the pleasant afternoon and evening in his father's apartment, Adam's announcement that they were going "out on the town" the next night, filled Molly's heart with dread. What would she wear? She had never been "out on the town," whatever that was. She only knew that she didn't want to go, and desperately wished that she was back home in the bush. *This time I'll really make a fool of myself,* she thought desperately. The thoughts whirled around in her head, but one stayed with her. She would phone Herb Belsile and ask for money to buy a suitable dress and wrap. She drifted off to sleep with that idea in mind.

When morning came, she waited impatiently until it was time for Herb to be in his office, then waited until she could use the telephone privately. The time came, finally. The housekeeper was in the kitchen and Adam went into his bedroom and closed the door. She hastened to the phone, looked up Herb's number, and dialed.

It was a blessed relief when she heard the familiar voice on the line! He wasted valuable time making pleasantries,

121

and after assuring him she was well, she told him she needed money to buy clothes.

"How much do you need, Molly? You have a balance in your bank in Fairbanks."

"I know, Herb, but that's only a small balance. I'd like to have several months' allowance deposited here in Anchorage that I can use today." She kept her voice low.

"I'll arrange it for you." He told her the bank he would use and advised her to sign the checks with her married name, Molly Reneau. Then he asked if there was anything else she would like to discuss with him.

"No, Herb, I'm doing fine, and I appreciate the money. I won't be needing an allowance, now, for several months." After a few more pleasantries were exchanged, she rang off.

When she turned, Adam was barring her way.

She gasped! "I didn't know you were there."

"I'll bet you didn't. What was that all about?"

She took a deep breath and turned her face up to meet his accusing stare.

"I was talking to Herb Belsile."

"I know who you were talking to. I was going to use the phone in the bedroom, and I heard you."

"You listened!" she said accusingly.

"Not on the phone. I came out here and listened."

Pride, and then anger came to her defense. "I was talking to my attorney about money. Is there anything else you'd like to know?" After the sleepless night her nerves were on edge and she wanted to get away from him before she disgraced herself and cried.

"Why do you need several months' allowance?" he asked bluntly.

"You've no right to know about my financial affairs any more than I have the right to know about yours, Adam Reneau."

122

"You think not, Molly Reneau?" he said sharply. "You're my wife. You know what that means? It means that I'm responsible for you whether you like it or not."

Her mouth compressed. Before she could give a suitable retort, his voice softened, he let his hands go up and down her arms in a caressing motion, and he continued:

"You're worried about going out tonight and want to buy new clothes."

The amazement showed in her eyes before her glance fell. "Now you know all my little secrets."

He made a kind of growling noise in his throat and tried to pull her toward him, but she resisted. "It isn't so important what you wear, Molly."

"It is to me," she replied.

He pulled her to him and hugged her. "We'll go out and buy you the best-looking outfit in town, if that's what you want."

She pushed herself away from him. "It isn't what I want, Adam! I'll buy my own clothes, thank you."

He gave a sharp exclamation and his black brows drew together. "Not with me, you won't! I'd look like a fool."

"You don't need to go alone." She knew she shouldn't have said it. She saw the determination flash in his eyes and knew her case was lost.

"I'm going! I'm paying! If you're such a square about your husband buying your clothes, you can pay me back."

For a long moment she didn't move. The expression on her features was easy to read; the doubt, indecision, and then resignation as she came to a decision.

"All right, but only if I pay back every cent. I'm not a charity case. My father left me provided for."

She was standing determinedly, trying so hard to be independent. A sudden desire came over Adam to cherish her. He looked at the trembling mouth and wanted to kiss it. Not the brotherly kisses he had been giving it, but the passionate kisses of a man who wants to make love to a woman. He knew he dared not, so he casually said, "You win. We'll do it your way this time." He could see the apprehension on Molly's face and was surprised at himself for trying so desperately to put her at ease.

CHAPTER ELEVEN

Molly's apprehension escalated the moment they stepped into the fashionable dress shop where they had come to buy her clothes.

The room they entered was pale green with touches of white. The deep carpet, white sofas, long glass tables, and potted plants gave the impression of an elegant sitting room. A tall, slender, fashionably dressed woman came to meet them.

"Adam!" She gave him an electric smile and held out her hands. "How nice to see you." He took her outstretched hands.

"And nice to see you, Jaclyn." His voice was cool, and he dropped her hands after only a brief contact.

The woman stood there smiling, seemingly unaware of the rebuff, which was apparent to Molly. She sensed, immediately, the aloofness that had come over Adam. She wished desperately he hadn't come with her and fidgeted nervously. She felt gawky and uncomfortable standing beside him looking up at this tall, chic woman.

"This is my wife." Adam turned to her and took her hand.

Jaclyn turned astonished eyes to Molly. "Your wife?" "You? Married?" There was no mistaking the amusement and disbelief in her voice.

Her eyes swung to Molly and surveyed her with unsmiling curiosity. She took her time assessing her, missing nothing. The scrutiny went on for so long that Molly felt acutely embarrassed. Adam seemed to be amused.

"Well," Jaclyn said at last, "her figure is good, although she's rather short."

Molly's blood was boiling; her anger was directed at Adam as well as the woman. How dare he bring her here to be looked at, judged, and have her imperfections pointed out to him. Her mouth opened, but before she could frame a suitable retort, he squeezed her hand to silence her.

"The reason we're here is to select a wardrobe for my beautiful wife. I don't wish to spoil her natural beauty. I know exactly how she should be dressed—with very little sophistication, do you agree?" His tone was cool and oddly patronizing.

"Of course you're right, Adam. You've always had excellent taste . . . in clothes," she said grudgingly.

"Take us to one of your rooms and show us evening dresses and wraps."

When they were seated in a small mirrored room and Jaclyn had left them alone, Molly turned on him.

"I don't like any part of this," she fumed. "I'll not be looked over like I was a . . . horse!"

Adam smiled down into her angry face. The violet eyes sparkled with indignation. He chuckled softly and put his arm around her.

"She's a professional, Molly, that's why we came here. Whether you like her or not she knows clothes and, remember, you're the one that wanted to be suitably dressed."

"I don't care," she sputtered, "I still don't—"

"If you don't shut up, I'm going to kiss you." He tried to appear very stern. Molly got only so far as to open her mouth when his came down on it and stopped the words and all thoughts of words. He kissed her long and hard, not the little kisses he had been giving her, but the same kisses he gave her on that night she almost lost her head. Her heart was beating wildly when he finally raised his head. His eyes had narrowed and his breath was coming a little faster. A wild thought came to Molly. *He enjoyed kissing me as much as I enjoyed being kissed!*

They both looked up to see the woman, Jaclyn, watching them with a look of annoyance on her face. Molly felt a wave of pure exultation. *The woman was jealous! Well,* she thought spitefully, *that paid her back for the snippy remark about my height.*

"If you're ready, Adam," she said, in what Molly believed to be her professional tone, "we'll show you what I think would be suitable for your . . ."—there was a short, meaningful pause—". . . wife."

Models began to appear as if from nowhere in response to the command from Jaclyn. They displayed one gorgeous creation after the other. Molly's head began to swim in her efforts to choose from the collection of clothes that were paraded before her. Without objection she accepted Adam's choice and went with Jaclyn to the fitting rooms.

The dress she, or rather Adam, chose was cut from white velvet. The bodice folded itself lovingly around her young breasts. It as well as the tiny stand-up collar was studded with rhinestones. The skirt fell quite straight and simple to her feet. She loved it and thought it must cost the earth, but three months' allowance should cover the cost of the dress and the long white wool coat. The seamstress took her measurements while she was undressed. The evening dress would be shortened and she assured Molly she would be able to wear it that evening.

The shopping had not been the ordeal Molly feared. Coming back to the small room where Adam was waiting she found him standing with Jaclyn viewing clothing brought in by models, who after holding up the garment for his inspection, would wait until he shook his head either up and down or sideways. Jaclyn was busy with a

127

pad and pencil. The clothing ran from skirts and sweaters to day dresses to slack suits and loungewear.

Desperation made Molly's voice sharper than she intended it to be.

"Adam!" She clutched his sleeve. "Adam, what—"

"Just a minute, darling," he cut her off.

"What . . ." The agitation in her voice caused him to turn and whisper in her ear.

"Shut up, or I'll kiss you again."

"I can't afford this stuff!" she hissed.

Adam turned back to Jaclyn as if she hadn't spoken.

"Deliver these things to my apartment, Jaclyn, and add a supply of underthings." Then to Molly's utter consternation he added, "And see to it there are some negligees and nighties included and . . . ah . . . be sure one is black lace."

He squeezed her hand so tightly she thought he would break the bones. She was mortified! She had been stripped naked here in front of this woman as if she were a store window mannequin! All her instincts urged her to tell them both off; instead, she walked sedately beside Adam to the door. There, Jaclyn spoke the only words she had said to her since they had entered her shop.

"I hope you enjoy your new wardrobe . . . Mrs. Reneau."

Molly's head went up and with it shrewishness she didn't know she possessed.

"It will do . . . for now, Jaclyn. Thank you for showing us your collection." With all the dignity of a queen she marched ahead of Adam and out the door.

When they reached the street, it was a different matter. In no uncertain terms she let him know that she was not having all those clothes.

"I can't afford them. The dress and wrap will take my allowance for three months!" She ended on a pleading note: "And another thing, that woman didn't believe we 'were married, She thought you had picked me up and was . . ."

"Was . . . what?" he laughed. "She thought you were my mistress! Wouldn't she be surprised if she knew the truth?"

"You let her think . . . it," she snapped bitterly.

"I don't care what she thinks, Molly mine." He tucked her hand into his and put both their hands in his coat pocket.

"I'll call Herb and tell him I'll need more money," Molly said dejectedly.

"No, you won't. You can pay me back when the year ends. Now let's hear no more about it." He was walking so fast she was almost trotting to keep up with him.

In the late afternoon Molly lay down on the big wide bed in her room and tried to doze off, but her mind was too active. Her eyes wandered around the room, her room, temporarily. She wondered who had used the room and left the lipstick. She shied away from thoughts of Adam being with a woman. The quiet of the room began to have its effect and her eyes became heavy with sleep. The sleepless night and the shopping tour had taken a toll of the strength she had gained after her bout with the flu. She turned over on her side, tucked her hands under her cheek, and slept.

She awoke an hour later feeling amazingly refreshed and went into the bathroom to run her bath. From the array of toiletries assembled on the shelf beneath the large mirror she selected the liquid bubble bath and generously doused her bath water. The result delighted her. The tub filled with soft bubbles emitting a haunting fragrance. She luxuriated in the big square tub, loath to get out. The steam from the bath had allowed a few tendrils of her hair to escape the hairpins she had used to pin it up. She was raising up out of the tub to reach more pins when she heard her bedroom door open.

Through her half-open bathroom door she saw Adam walk into her bedroom with his arms piled with boxes which he dumped on the bed. She gasped in dismay. His laughing dark eyes met her startled ones, traveled down over her bare shoulders, then deliberately lower. He walked into the bathroom and seated himself on a stool. Molly was shocked speechless.

"Want me to wash your back?" he asked drolly. She tried to sink lower into the bubbles.

"You're being a smartass, Adam! Get out of here!"

He reached for a washcloth, dipped it in the water, and let it trail across the back of her neck.

"Nasty words! I'll have to wash your mouth out with soap." He whispered in her ear then nipped the lobe gently with his teeth.

She grabbed the cloth and was about to swing with it when he jumped out of the way.

"Go ahead with your bath, kitten. I'll unpack your dress."

Molly sank lower in the tub and prayed the bubbles would last until he left the room. She could see him unpacking the white dress and hanging it on a hanger. To her chagrin he unpacked everything. The lacy underthings, the nightgowns. He laid out high-heeled silver sandals she had not seen before. He rummaged in the boxes and came toward the bathroom with an infuriating devilish grin on his face. He was holding up for her inspection a sheer black lace negligee.

"Here's something for you to put on when you get out of the tub," he drawled.

"Get out of here, Adam Reneau!" she said crossly, and threw the wet cloth at him. He dodged it easily and came to kneel down beside the tub.

"You shouldn't throw things at your husband," he scolded.

She could feel his breath on her cheek. His hand went

130

out to cra⁻le the back of her head. She was looking into his eyes when his lips came down on hers. His kiss was light until her lips parted voluntarily then it deepened, his breath quickened, and he pulled her to him, lifting her wet arm out of the water to guide it around his neck. His hand caressed her bare back and coming around cupped and squeezed her small pointed breasts that were half concealed by the bubbles. She felt an electric current going through her. He tore his mouth from hers and buried his face in the damp, fragrant skin of her neck.

"Do you know what you're doing to me?" he demanded huskily, and not waiting for an answer, he gently pulled down her lower lip with his thumb and forefinger and fastened his lean mouth to hers again.

Molly had never been kissed by any other man and even he had never kissed her in this savage, passionate way before. She arched toward him, pliant in his arms. Only a small part of her consciousness urged her to try and stop him.

His dark eyes were glazed with emotion when he lifted his head. Aroused as she was Molly hardly knew when his lips had left hers. He kissed her on the nose then gently drew her arm from around his neck. Scooping up a handful of bubbles he covered her pink-tipped breasts where they rose out of the water.

"Am I the only man to have kissed you?"

She nodded, not taking her eyes from his. She felt as if she was mesmerized. He placed little nibbly kisses on her face and neck.

"You are precious, Molly mine." He got to his feet and without looking at her went out and closed the door.

Molly sat perfectly still for some minutes after he left, showing no trace of the emotion chasing through her veins. Why didn't she feel any shame for allowing him to caress her as he had? The way her body responded to his caresses frightened her. She shook her wandering thoughts together and got out of the tub.

Toweling herself dry and generously dusting herself with talcum powder, she picked up the black lace garment Adam had dropped on the floor. It was lovely and she couldn't resist trying it on. She opened the door and peeked into the bedroom before going in. She was sure he wouldn't be there, but she was taking no chances. She shed the sheer robe for a more practical one and gave herself up to the pleasure of looking over her new wardrobe.

Molly dressed slowly for her evening out with Adam. She needed the self-confidence of knowing she looked her best. The new gown and coat would certainly help. She had no idea of what Adam's mood would be. She was nervous at the thought of meeting him after the scene in the bathroom.

She stood back from the mirror to judge the finished effect and wondered at the miracle fashionable clothes could achieve. The sleeveless bodice, with the small mandarin collar, the straight skirt, and the high-heeled sandals were a perfect foil for her slender young figure. Makeup was minimal—a touch of blue eye shadow to highlight her eyes, a smear of coral lipstick to outline a mouth made vulnerable by the fullness of the lower lip, and a dusting of powder gave a mat appearance to the small straight nose. She had brushed her hair until it shone, and knowing Adam's aversion to having it pinned, had left it hang to her shoulders, the ends slightly turning up. She was gazing unbelievingly into the mirror at the elegant stranger when, after a rap on the door, Adam walked in.

Molly's pulse began to race as he looked her over from the top of her head to the tips of her silver shoes peeking out from under the white dress. Twin fires lit his dark, exciting eyes and Molly waited breathlessly for him to speak.

He came to stand behind her, his eyes holding hers in

132

the reflection of the mirror. He put his hands on her bare arms.

"So beautiful, and so damned unaware of it!" He turned her around to face him and fondled the diamond earrings she had fastened to her ears.

He looked particularly handsome in the dark suit; the whiteness of his shirt contrasted with the darkness of his skin. His black hair had been brushed into place, but was already rebelling against the direction it had been forced to go. His brilliant dark eyes never moved from her face while he stood strangely silent. Molly felt her pulses warm her body as his appreciative gaze wandered over her. The force of her emotions deepened the color of her eyes, the most piquant feature of her beauty.

"You have lovely eyes, Molly mine," he murmured, his eyes lingering on her face.

Molly, obeying a totally reckless impulse, held up her face to him. His lips tilted slightly as he bent his dark head and kissed her on the nose.

"I've promised Dad he could see his lovely daughter before we go." His beautiful voice turned her heart over. He picked up her white coat and laid it over his arm and they left the apartment.

Adam stopped the car outside a tall gray building. A private club, he told her as he hurried her into the warmth of the building. After tossing his car keys to a warmly dressed doorman they removed their wraps and entered the dining room. It seemed all eyes were focused upon them as they paused in the doorway. The men looked appreciatively at the lovely girl, and the women openly eyed the handsome man beside her.

Adam was evidently well known here. The headwaiter called him by name when he showed them to a table. As they seated themselves, the orchestra began to play. The music was soft and romantic and one or two couples got up to dance on the small dance floor.

"I hope you like salmon," Adam said. "I took the liberty of ordering our meal in advance."

Molly nodded, trying desperately not to be nervous. She looked around the room at the fashionably dressed, sophisticated women who were perfectly comfortable in these surroundings. This was Adam's world. He was at ease here. A little wave of depression hit her.

Adam ordered a bottle of champagne with their meal, and as they waited for their first course to arrive, she sipped it cautiously, remembering the effect it had had on her when she had first drunk it at their wedding reception. He laughed at her and smiled a sweet, almost loving smile.

When she had almost finished what was in her glass, he filled it up again. She began to feel wonderfully gay and chattered to him all through their meal. He responded with a mood to match hers and she thought she had never been so happy.

To the curious onlookers they presented a picture of two people completely engrossed in each other. Adam's eyes never left her face and it was plain to see the lovely girl adored him.

Charlie had taught Molly to dance when she first went to the bush to live, but she had danced only with him and a few times with Jim Robinson at a club in Fairbanks. Adam asked her to dance and was pleasantly surprised when she got to her feet. The dance floor was small and dimly lit and when they began to dance, he was glad that she melted into his arms without a trace of nervousness. Their steps matched perfectly as they moved slowly around the floor to the romantic music the orchestra was playing. He rested his cheek on the top of her head. Molly was so enchanted by the magic of it all that she was afraid to speak in case the spell would be broken. She relaxed against him, oblivious of everyone. They lost themselves in the enchantment of their first dance together.

The music stopped and Adam smiled down at her. With

his arm still around her waist they made their way back to their table. Couples from the nearby tables watched them leave the dance floor. Some called out greetings to Adam as they passed. He nodded coolly to each one who spoke, but declined to stop and they proceeded on to the alcove and their table.

He had seated Molly and was about to seat himself when a voice from behind him spoke his name. Molly looked up to see a girl so incredibly beautiful that she blinked. She was as dark haired as Adam, but her skin was a soft mat whiteness. Bright red lipstick covered her pouting lips and her voluptuously rounded figure was dressed to perfection in a revealing black gown that showed a large expanse of her body.

"Hello, Wanita," Adam said, nodding to her escort who stood several paces behind her. The girl moved up close to Adam and linked her arm with his.

Molly looked from the girl to Adam. He was wearing his reticent expression, and his lips had a sardonic twist.

"I've missed you, Adam." The voice was soft, seductive.

"I find that hard to believe, Wanita," Adam said sarcastically, disengaging his arm from her hold. "If you'll excuse me, my wife and I are enjoying a twosome this evening."

Wanita stared at him, not bothering to hide her anger. As the silence lengthened she swung her large blue eyes around at Molly and her lips curled. She looked back at Adam, venom in her eyes.

"You married *her*?" There was no mistaking the sardonic emphasis she put on her words. Molly cringed. Adam didn't even bother to answer and the angry eyes swung back to Molly.

"Get you pregnant, did he?" she sneered. "An old pro like you should never have let that happen, Adam." Her fiery gaze turned on him.

"Good-bye, Wanita." Adam pulled out his chair and sat

135

down. Neither said anything for a while after the girl left. Molly's arm was resting on the table and Adam laid his hand on it as they sat in silence.

"I'm sorry, Molly," he said finally.

She tried to smile naturally, but the smile never reached her eyes as she thought of Wanita's cruel insinuation. She found herself replying, saying it didn't matter in the least, trying to hide her pain. His hand on her arm moved back and forth in a caressing motion. He looked at her smiling lips and pleading eyes and his grin came back. His hand slid down her arm and his fingers interlaced with hers.

"Molly mine, you're precious! Shall we go back to the apartment and have a private party all our own?"

She nodded eagerly, trying to quell the deep sorrow welling inside her. "I might even get tipsy!" she said brightly. He chuckled at the thought.

When they left the dining room, his arm was around her.

The gay mood stayed with them all the way back to the apartment. While she was hanging up her coat Adam brought out a bottle of champagne and encased it in a bucket of ice. He was selecting records for the stereo when she came back into the room. He looked up, saw her, and held out his hand. She went to him. He was in a strange mood tonight. He seemed to want to touch her, and she wanted him to.

She was feeling relaxed and a lot happier now. The soft glow of the lamps and the sensuous music added to the feeling of time suspended. Adam's dark eyes had developed a mild look of teasing and at the same time she was sure he felt desire for her. She was grateful he found her desirable enough to want to make love to her. *This was enough for now,* she thought. If the fates were kind, maybe love would come later.

"May I have this dance?" he asked formally, taking the glass from her hand. They had toasted each other with two glasses of champagne and it had began to lend its own particular magic to the evening.

She went into his arms. "Just this one. I'm booked up for the rest of the evening."

"Lucky man." They were moving slowly. He lifted first one of her arms and then the other up onto his shoulders. She needed no other encouragement to clasp them around his neck. He wrapped both arms around her and they swayed together.

"I've never danced like this," she murmured, pressing her face to his shoulder.

He moved his hand down to her hips and pulled her even closer. "Well, I should hope not!"

"I think I'm a little bit tipsy, Adam."

"Hmmmm . . . I think so."

"Do you mind?"

"Not as long as you're with me."

"Would you mind if I was a little bit tipsy with someone else?" Her voice was taking on a dreamy quality.

"I would mind like hell if you were with anyone else."

"You would?" she said wonderingly. "Oh!"

"Oh, what?"

"Oh, I didn't know you would care if I got a little bit tipsy with someone else . . . Adam?"

"Hmmm . . ."

"Have you made love to a lot of women?"

"A few."

"Did you love them?"

"No. I made love to them, but I didn't love them."

"That wasn't very nice. I'd never do that."

"Do what?"

"Let men make love to me. I want just one man and I want him to want just me. I want him to love me."

He didn't answer. He encircled her neck with one large hand and tilted her chin up with his thumb. Her eyes were tightly closed, and as he looked at her, two crystal tears squeezed themselves out from under the dark lashes. Her mouth trembled and she tried to bury her face in his shoulder again.

"Darling? Molly," he said huskily, his hand going to the nape of her neck and pressing her head to him.

"I've had a little too much to drink!" Her voice was muffled against him.

He caught her up into his arms, carried her across to the couch, sat down, and cuddled her against him.

"Don't cry, love." His lips tasted the salty tears on her face. He rocked her back and forth and crooned to her. "Darling, don't cry!" He kissed her, not with passionate kisses, but with loving tender ones, from her eyes to her lips to her throat.

"I've had a little too much to drink." She said it again and even to her own intoxicated self it was a lame-sounding excuse. But it was so wonderful being here with him!

They sat silently. He rested his cheek against her forehead and she snuggled her face against his throat. Her arm was around his shoulders and her fingers gently stroked the nape of his neck. The music played on and he caressed her and soothed her, content just to hold her.

Molly stirred and tilted her head back so she could look up. "Adam . . . ?"

"Yes, love?"

"May I kiss you?" she whispered, as her hand came around to the side of his face.

"I'd like that, love."

She pulled his face to hers and gently kissed his lips. He kept perfectly still and she kissed his face, the corner of his mouth, his cheeks, his chin, any part of his face she could reach. Then sighing she turned her face again to his throat. She could feel him trembling now and his heart, against her breast, was beating rapidly.

"Adam, . . . will you ever sleep with me again?" In her

intoxicated state the question seemed to be a reasonable one.

"That would be up to you."

"Do you want to?" she persisted.

"You know I do," he whispered huskily.

"Would you tonight, if I asked?"

"No, love, not tonight. The champagne's talking, not you."

"Yes, you're right, Adam." The muffled voice drifted off.

Adam sat for a while longer and held the sleeping girl. He smoothed the hair back from her forehead and removed the diamond earrings. Reaching down he slipped the silver sandals from her feet. He gazed at her face and his life, up to now, raced before his eyes. *How many women out there were worth the trouble to run after? Wanita was a good example of what there was to choose from,* he thought bitterly. He kissed the parted lips once more, resisting the urge to crush her to him. Slowly and carefully he got to his feet and carried her down the hall to her room.

CHAPTER TWELVE

Molly awakened next morning and lay for a moment wondering where she was, surprised by the silence. She turned her head and looked at the clock and remembered.

A flood of memories came rushing in, tumbling over each other. Memories of dancing with Adam, of kissing him and wanting more. *Oh, God!* What had she done and said? Not wanting to dwell on these memories that made her feel guilty for desiring a man who didn't want her, she swung out of bed and stood looking down at herself. She had on a violet chiffon nightie and that was all! She gave a despairing little cry! As the heat of her embarrassment flooded her, she took a deep breath and looked about the room. Her dress of last evening lay over a chair, her undergarments tossed nearby. She faintly remembered asking Adam if she could kiss him. How could she have done such a thing? She would never drink another intoxicating drink as long as she lived, she vowed.

The new clothes were hanging in the wardrobe. The housekeeper must have put them away while they were out last evening. She quickly chose a pair of light green wool pants and fluffy sweater to match and slid into them, surprised at the perfect fit. She brushed her hair and looked closely at her face in the mirror. Gazing at herself, she wondered how she could have been so naive to think a man like Adam could desire that reflection in the mirror. She sighed deeply and swept her hair back and secured it with a ribbon, scolding herself silently for indulging in fantasy.

She started for the kitchen, then remembered the diamond earrings. Turning back to the dressing table she looked under and around everything on the table. They were not there. *Oh, God!* Had she lost them? She went to the living room and searched the floor near where the silver sandals lay. Desperately she went to the kitchen to find the housekeeper. Ganson was there packing boxes.

"Hello. So you finally got up, did you?"

"Good morning. I'm so worried, Ganson, I can't find the earrings Mr. Reneau gave me. I've looked everywhere!" Her voice rose in desperation.

At that moment Adam came through the swinging door. "Looked everywhere for what?"

"I've lost the earrings!" she blurted out.

"You haven't lost them. I have them in my pocket."

Relief flowed through her. She went to him and leaned her forehead against his chest. "Thank you. I was so afraid."

"I took them off when you went to sleep last night." The color came into her cheeks as the memory of the pile of clothes flashed through her mind. "Eat your breakfast. We'll be leaving soon."

Adam sat the plane down on the frozen lake. He had been silent on the trip back. Molly glanced at him with anxious eyes hoping to see some sign that he was glad to be back, but his face was expressionless.

The weather was changing; there was tension in the air; heavy clouds formed in the east. The sun was already low by the time the plane was anchored, and a circle of silvery light sprang around it. Within this large loop, four shining circles appeared. In each circle, a small, unreal but gleaming image of the sun shone. Looking up at the five tangent suns gave Molly a weird and alien feeling. The silver circles became hazy, the mock suns flashed evilly, the daylight seemed to flicker, and the vision vanished. The true sun sank into the dark clouds.

"You've seen the sun dogs," Adam said, helping her out of the plane. An icy blast of air hit her and his words were almost lost in the wind. "Ten to one we'll have a blizzard by morning."

Molly knew that to be true. The Indians were afraid of the sun dogs, thinking they were evil stars trying to kill the sun. They would beat pans and raise an awful racket trying to scare them away.

It was almost totally dark by the time they trudged through the snow to the house. Tim-Two had shoveled a path, but it was filling fast with drifting snow. Adam went to the shed for the snowmobile and sled so he could bring the supplies from the plane. Molly wanted to help, but he hustled her into the house and firmly closed the door.

She was glad to be home again. This is where she belonged. She let her hands run lovingly over the fireplace mantel, opened the glass door of the clock, and started winding the spring. The rhythmic ticking of the clock gave her the feeling of continuance and peace. After lighting the lamps she set about the chore of putting her city things away.

It was snowing heavily by the time Adam returned with the last load of supplies. He was tired, cold, and very hungry. Molly handed him a cup of coffee and quietly went about cooking their supper. When it was ready, he came to the table and ate automatically.

Abruptly he said, in a strangely husky voice, "It's going to be a long winter, Molly."

She stiffened at the sound of those familiar words, dropped her eyes, and stared at her plate attempting to hide her feeling of depression.

"Yes," she said slowly, and pushed herself away from

the table to walk to the fireplace, her hands clasped fearfully in front of her.

Adam finished his supper and carried the dishes to the sink, then filled his cup with coffee and sat down in the big chair, studying her rigid back. When he spoke again, it was in a more normal tone.

"You can't stand up all winter, Molly, so sit down and relax."

Her shoulders drooped suddenly as she acknowledged the truth of his words. She relaxed even more and turned to him.

"If I did anything to offend you last evening, I'm sorry." Her voice was defensive. "Not being used to drinking much, I—"

"You did nothing to be embarrassed about, Molly." After hesitating a moment he added, "Do you have regrets?"

The evening was not as companionable as other evenings had been. Adam sat quietly in his chair. Molly rocked in hers and listened to the howl of the wind around the cabin.

Adam interrupted the silence by saying, "I better get to bed, there'll be a lot of snow to shovel in the morning."

Molly nodded, and got to her feet. "Good night."

"Good night, Molly."

Adam went out after breakfast the next morning to check on the ski plane. The wind had subsided some, but the snow was still falling. The atmosphere inside the cabin was easier this morning, and Molly went about her duties with an air of acceptance. She chided herself time and again for her illusive dreams. Although his dark eyes had followed her as she prepared breakfast, she sensed a tightness in him that had not been there before.

She was washing dishes when Adam came dashing through the kitchen door.

"I need the gun, Molly!" He snatched it from the wall

143

over the fireplace. Checking its load, he made again for the door.

Molly ran after him. "What is it? What's the matter?"

"Wolverine. He's been in Tim-Two's traps and we can smell him near the shed." Molly lingered beside the door. Adam stopped in front of her. "I want you to shut this door and stay inside. Do you understand?"

She nodded, shut the door, and went to the window. Dog was running about, barking excitedly. *Dear God, don't let Adam be hurt. Please, please, please!* "I love him." She said the words aloud unaware of doing so. Without a thought of Adam's orders she slipped into her parka, stepped into her snow boots, and went out the door.

Taking big frosty breaths of the chilling air she knew the foul-smelling beast was close by as soon as she stepped out the door. Rounding the corner of the house she could see Dog holding the small wolverine at bay between the shed and the board fence. She heard the savage growling as the snarling beast lunged at Dog. Molly knew Dog didn't have a chance and screamed at him. He backed off as the undaunted wolverine charged him. Adam dropped to one knee in the snow, aimed the gun, and squeezed the trigger.

The shot hit the wolverine dead center and he dropped into a convulsing heap. Dog charged in, but was reluctant to touch the foul-smelling body. Molly called him and he obediently came to her.

Adam rose and swung around to face her. "I told you to stay in the cabin!" he shouted harshly.

"I know you did, but I was worried for Dog . . . and you." Her voice quavered in her relief that he was safe.

"You risked your life!" He yelled at her in his anger.

"I didn't think I was risking my life," she said in way of defense.

"The odds were not in your favor with the wolverine. If he'd got past me, he would have been at your throat in a second." He was so angry now his face had turned red.

Her lips quivered as she realized the danger to Adam as well as to herself. If he had been distracted for even one second by her appearance . . . she shivered and dropped her eyes, abandoning her defense.

"Get inside!" he commanded.

She hurried into the cabin, shut the door, and leaned against it, weak at the thought of what she had done. She could hear Adam and Tim-Two discussing the wolverine.

"By damm, by damm!" Tim-Two was saying. "What a devil! Him would come right to the cabin, no?"

Adam stayed away from the cabin most of the day. He and Tim-Two tried to rid the place of the smell of the beast. He helped the Indian disenfect his traps; otherwise he would have no winter catch. All animals shy away from the smell of the wolverine. Molly suspected he was staying away so his temper would cool before confronting her again.

Darkness set in before he returned. The cabin was filled with the tantalizing odor of cooking meat and vegetables. He sniffed approvingly.

"Something smells good," he said.

She gave a pleased little smile, but avoided meeting his eyes. She knew that he knew his favorite dish was a peace offering.

She served him the stew and hot biscuits. After being out in the cold most of the day he was hungry and had several helpings. His mood had softened, but she kept her eyes down, not wanting to give him an opening to speak about what had happened. Adam realized this and kept silent.

He was restless and wandered around the room while she was at the sink. She was frantically trying to plan something to do when she finished the dishes. It would be unbearable to sit across from him tonight if they didn't talk. She finished and was hanging away the towel when he came up close behind her. He put his hands on her

145

forearms and pulled her back against him. She could feel the thud of his heart—or was it her heart—she couldn't tell which. Leaning his head down he nuzzled her ear.

"You do understand why I was so angry?" She nodded. "I was terrified at what could have happened to you!"

She didn't say anything. She wanted to say she was sorry, but she couldn't get the words out.

Still holding her, he let his mouth rest on the side of her neck. "You'll not disobey me again, when I tell you to do something for your own good?"

"No. And I'm sorry," she whispered, her voice breaking.

He let out a long breath and squeezed her arms tightly. "Let's put on some music and sit by the fire, okay?" He took her hand and led her into the living area.

Molly sat in her rocker and watched him while he loaded the stereo with the music he had selected. She filled her eyes with him, the broad shoulders, the narrow waist, the lean hips. *I'll always love him,* she thought. *How could I possibly love another man after knowing him?* She picked up her knitting, so she would have something to do with her hands and have an excuse for not looking at him.

He came to his big chair, sat down, and stretched out his long legs. He was so still Molly thought he had fallen asleep, so she dared a look at him. His black eyes were openly staring at her. She held his gaze for a moment, then dropped her eyes, the color coming up into her cheeks. She saw the long legs draw up out of her line of vision. He got up and came toward her, took the knitting out of her hands, and put it on the floor by her chair. Taking her hand in his he drew her to her feet, and drawing her along with him went back to his chair and sat down. He tugged at her hand, but she resisted him. He tugged harder and pulled her down onto his lap.

He settled himself comfortably after swinging her legs across the arm of the chair and pressing her head down

146

on his shoulder. Molly attempted to raise her head and look at him, but he pressed her head firmly down again.

"Be still," he said, "I just want to hold you."

They listened to the music, much the same as they did the night in Adam's apartment. Molly snuggled closer in his arms and gave herself up to the joy of being close to him. He was in a strangely quiet mood. He stroked her hair and ran his fingers down the smooth flesh of her arm. She timidly lifted her fingers to his neck, then to his ear, coming to his cheek to find his mouth and trace it lightly. She felt his lips open and nibble at her fingers. She smiled a seret smile against his throat. She loved him, she wanted him, and he wasn't indifferent to her. The knowledge gave her the courage to allow her fingers to stray to the buttons on his shirt and slip her hand inside the opening to touch his skin. The hair on his chest was slightly rough against her fingers and she felt a shudder go through him as she gently tugged at it.

His lips decended to hers where they teased lightly, sending curious sensations along Molly's spine, and coherent thought slid into oblivion. She gave a convulsive shudder and put her arms about his neck signaling her complete submission with parted lips. His mouth crushed down on hers, demanding, hurting, and pleasing her. She felt the warmth of his body and the beat of his heart beneath her palms. He forced back her head and deepened the kiss to hot, insistent possession. She made no move to stop him when he unbuttoned her blouse, and his fingers teased the stiff nipples, caressing them so that they hardened even more. Every part of her body ached with the need of him. The little sounds she made seemed to arouse him more and he trembled violently and slid his lips from her mouth to her cheek then down to her neck.

"Darling . . ." His voice was husky and almost inaudible. He buried his face in her neck. She could feel his lips and tongue. Her body was on fire for him and she felt as if she were suspended in outer space.

Adam lifted his head and his half-closed eyes flashed over her face. His was strangely pale.

"I thought I could hold you and not make love to you, but I can't," he said hoarsely. He lifted her from his lap and got to his feet. "Go to bed, Molly."

She looked at him dazedly, her trembling fingers working at the buttons on her blouse. With bowed head and on shaking legs, she went to her room. She was on the point of tears, tired and drained.

Molly stood in the darkened room for a few minutes before turning up the light and making ready for bed. There was an ache in the pit of her stomach. In her innocence she didn't realize aroused desire was a tortuous thing. It was twisting inside her now like a small trapped animal, clawing for its freedom. Automatically she put several pieces of hardwood in the round stove and went into the bathroom where she brushed her teeth and washed her face. The cool cloth felt good on her burning skin. When leaving, she did as she did every night, opened the door to Adam's room, and closed the door to her own. She slipped on her nightgown. Sitting on the side of her bed she brushed her hair and words that had been etched into her subconscious filled her thoughts. Someday, Charlie had told her, a man will come into your life who will fill it with his presence. He will love and cherish you and give you children. When that time comes, it will be the beginning of an extension of yourself. Molly sat very still. The tension left her. She had reached a decision. After turning out the light she opened the kitchen door and slipped into bed.

The wind had gone down and the reflection of the white snow coming in the windows gave the room a soft glow. There were stirrings now in the other room. Adam had put the big log on the fire, checked the doors, and let Dog out into the cold night. She heard him moving about in his room and then he came through the bathroom and closed the connecting door. She lay tense and waiting.

The moment came! He opened the door to her room so the heat could circulate.

"Adam . . . ?"

"You called me?" He came into the room, his flashlight beaming a path on the floor.

"Yes." She was trembling with unbelievable tension.

He sat on the edge of the bed. "Something wrong, Molly?"

"Adam . . ." she started again bravely. "I've been thinking about what you said. Although we both know this marriage isn't permanent, it's a marriage. There's no reason why it shouldn't be a real one. I'm—I'm willing to be a wife to you, if you want me." Her voice vibrated with emotion. He turned out the light. "I'll not hold onto you . . . you'll always be free to go." All her barriers were down; her pride was gone.

He saw that she was both desperate and uncertain, and also near tears.

"Are you sure?" he asked hoarsely.

She answered with only the slightest hesitation. "Yes, I'm sure."

Adam stood, took off his robe, and raised the blankets to slip in beside her. He could see the gleaming whiteness of her shoulders and breasts. He put his arms around her and held her tightly to him, one hand moving down her back, fingers lightly caressing. She went to him willingly and snuggled against him. She was trembling with relief and unbelievable happiness. She heard him catch his breath sharply as her bare breasts came in contact with his chest. Her arms went around him and she nibbled at his neck with her teeth, uncertain of what was expected of her.

"I don't know what to do," she said in shaking tones.

"What do you want to do, love?" His lips were against her forehead.

"I want to kiss you!"

"Well . . ." he said laughing softly, happily.

"Adam . . . Adam."

She whispered the words against his mouth. He caressed her with his lips, soothing her body with his hands. A wild, sweet enchantment rippled through her veins as his mouth moved over her cheek, down her throat, and onto her breast. The knowledge that he was not trying to rush her, holding his own passion in check, filled her heart with love for him.

"Molly, sweetheart . . . !" he murmured in her ear.

When it was over, she was filled with indescribable joy and contentment. He stroked her hair and kissed her. With all the honesty of her young heart she reached up to whisper against his cheek: "I love you. Have I made you happy?"

His mouth moved in search of her own. "Very happy!"

She cradled his dark head against her breasts, enjoying this new and wondrous sensation. She felt him in every pore of her body and in every beat of her heart. She was silent for a long while, then whispered in a voice filled with awe.

"I could never imagine how it would be. I'm glad it was you who showed me."

He propped himself up on one elbow. The pale oval of her face was framed in the golden hair strewn across the pillow.

"There is more, sweetheart, and for you it will only get better."

The words were said against her mouth as the warm urgency of his lips claimed hers, and he took her again to that heavenly oblivion where she was aware of only his warm body and urgent demands.

"Go to sleep now." His voice broke into her drowsy

conscience. He kissed her shoulder and neck and heard her sigh of contentment. He ran his hand lovingly down the full length of her body and she took it in hers and held it tightly to her breast.

Molly awoke first and lay on her side watching him sleep. The strong, finely chiseled lines and contours of his face were relaxed. His mouth was firm and beautifully molded. How gentle he had been with her! She had never thought that the consummation of marriage could be such a glorious thing. She had been carried away on a passionate tide of love for him, out of her depth and into a new and completely uncharted sea that contained only Adam and the overpowering love she had for him.

Not once, but many times during the night she had confessed her love for him. He seemed to like hearing her say it. He called her "love," but never one time said he loved her. Not even when he reached out for her the second time, then a third, and made ardent love to her all over again.

The desire to touch him was irresistible to her now, and she pushed her fingers gently through his hair. So thick and soft it was! He stirred and she withdrew her hand and hid it beneath the covers, but it was caught and held tightly. Black eyes, just inches away from her own were open and laughing into hers.

"What were you thinking, while you were looking at me?"

"You were awake?"

"I was watching you even before you awakened. What were you thinking?"

"I . . . was thinking that you must me hungry!"

He laughed and pressed his body down on hers. "In the position you're in, you couldn't have been thinking about food!"

She slid her arms around his neck, her hand coming

around to stroke his cheek. "Your face is rough," she said with uninhibited frankness.

"It usually is the first thing in the morning. You'll just have to get used to it." He kissed her soundly before burying his face between her shoulder and neck. She jumped as his teeth nipped her. "Get up and fix my breakfast, woman!"

"In my position you want me to think about food?"

"Well . . . on second thought . . ." his words were shut off as his lips found hers.

Everything was bright and beautiful. It had stopped snowing and the world was crisp and white. The trees hung heavy with new snow and Dog scurried around making tracks as he chased the birds foraging for food. Tim-Two was preparing to reset his trap lines and Dog was excited at the prospect of a trip into the woods. Adam brought a fresh supply of wood into the house from the woodpile. His feet made snowy tracks on the kitchen floor, and he laughed at the scolding Molly gave him.

She was radiant with happiness, her sparkling eyes seeking Adam's at every opportunity. She was full of contentment, and her voice carried an extra trill when she spoke to Jim on the radio later that morning.

"How about it, Molly girl? How about that, pretty Molly girl? Do you have a copy this morning?" Jim's voice came in loud and clear.

Molly picked up the microphone. "Of course I have a copy! How are you on this lovely day?"

"Lovely day? It must be about thirty below!" He gave a burr sound.

"I'm baking fresh cookies, Big Bird. Do you have time to drop in?"

"No time for a tea party today unless you need me."

"I don't need a thing, Jim," she said gaily. She looked up to see Adam standing in the doorway, and gave him her brightest smile.

"You're sure now?" Jim insisted.

"Things are just fine with us, Jim. Tell Evelyn and the boys hello. Adam and I are sorry you can't stop this trip. Try and make time on your next run."

"Will do. I'm about out of range, so will clear with you until the next time." His voice faded as he flew out of range. Molly didn't answer, she knew her voice wouldn't reach him.

CHAPTER THIRTEEN

The days that followed were wonderful and the nights more so. Molly was walking on a bright cloud of happiness. She wanted to be with Adam every minute of the day; to see him and touch him. He seemed to feel the same. Whenever she was near, his arms reached out for her, and their smiling eyes would catch and hold. Some days didn't have enough hours for them to say all they wanted to say to each other. Other days they were content just to be near and to touch. No words were necessary.

Molly never let her mind wander to the months ahead. She looked back once and thought about her father. She hoped he knew how happy she was and wondered if this was, indeed, his plan for her. They never spoke about the forced marriage, or the separation at the end of the year. In the evenings she would curl up in his lap and they would listen to the radio or just stare into the fire, until their desire for one another became so great, Adam would dump her off his lap and growl: "Get to bed, woman!"

They had been living in their new happiness for a week when their name was called on the "personal message" program during the noon broadcast.

"Attention, Adam Reneau," the announcer said, "you have visitors coming up on the morning train. Suggest you be at the track eleven A.M."

"That will be Patrick. I didn't expect him for a while yet."

Molly tried not to show her disappointment and dampen Adam's enthusiasm. But somehow she felt the end had come to her dream world. Another person to share her honeymoon? Her year with Adam? A feeling of jealousy toward this unknown Patrick flooded her.

Later that night in bed, after the hunger for each other had been appeased and she lay contentedly in his arms, he asked her if she was sorry that his friend was coming. What could she say? That she was terrified she was going to lose this precious closeness they shared? She couldn't tell him that, so she lied and said she didn't mind at all and his friend was welcome.

Adam took the snowmobile and the sled down to the tracks to meet the train. He and Patrick would ride it back. The sled was for the luggage. Before he left the cabin, he locked Molly in his arms and kissed her soundly. She wrapped her arms about his neck, reluctant to let him go.

He nipped her playfully on the chin. "Just a taste of you to take with me!"

Molly watched until he was beyond the big timber and out of sight. It was the end of her time alone with him. Before depression could set in she started preparations for lunch. Work was the therapy she needed. With lunch started she changed from her jeans and shirt to the light green slacks and sweater Adam had bought for her in Anchorage.

She was busy at the range and flushed from the heat of the oven when she heard voices on the porch. *Damn!* she thought. She had wanted to fix her face and hair before meeting Patrick. But when her startled eyes saw who was coming through the door, all thoughts of her appearance left her mind.

Dressed in a black snowmobile suit, her silver hair glistening as she removed the warm headgear, her blue eyes wide and innocent, her pink mouth twisted in a cheerful smile, was her cousin Donna.

"Molly! I've accepted your invitation. Mama said you wanted me to come out and since Patrick was coming on the train, I decided to come along with him. Won't this be fun? The four of us here together!" The voice coming from the beautifully shaped mouth was so friendly!

The silence that followed beat in Molly's ears while she stared at her cousin as if she had returned from the dead. She tried to ignore her pumping heart and steady her voice.

"Hello, Donna." Behind Donna was a man whose friendly eyes were staring at her. "You're Patrick." Her voice was calm even to her own ears.

"My wife, Molly." Adam came from behind the stranger.

Molly extended her hand and it was enveloped after he hastily removed his mitten. Patrick had a twinkle in his blue eyes, and a deeply tanned face under a thatch of sandy hair bleached by the Australian sun. He was not as tall or as heavy as Adam. Molly knew she would like him.

"I'm glad to meet you, Patrick." She wanted to smile at Adam's friend, but was afraid her face would crack with the effort. Desperately trying to stay calm she said to Adam, "Did you have room for the luggage?"

His expression was unreadable. "Yes. Pat had to ride the sled, but we made it. I'll bring it in."

"I'll help." Patrick went out the door behind him.

Molly's fingers curled into her palms and she turned to face Donna. There was a moment of fierce glaring between them.

"Why have you come?" she asked bluntly.

Donna unzipped her suit. The snow from her boots was melting and making puddles on the floor.

"I think you know." All the sweetness was gone from her voice.

156

"I didn't invite you. I don't want you here."

"I know you don't, but Adam does."

"I don't believe it."

Donna looked disinterested. "Ask him. Ask him when I was in his apartment last."

"I don't believe it!" Molly repeated, her cheeks scarlet.

Donna smiled cruelly. "Poor little Molly!" she mocked. "Don't tell me you've fallen for him!"

"I think you're here to cause trouble!" Molly was shaking now.

"What you think doesn't interest me in the least, cousin Molly," Donna snapped, then quickly turned to smile as Patrick came in the door carrying a large piece of luggage. Adam came in behind him carrying a heavier load.

Molly's burning cheeks welcomed the icy blast from the open door. Adam looked at her with a slightly puzzled expression on his face, but before he could speak, Donna came quickly forward and grasped his arm.

"Put my things in Molly's room, Adam. She says she has oodles of closet space." Her voice carried the purring tone again and her big blue eyes gazed up at him adoringly.

Adam hesitated only a moment before taking the cases to Molly's room.

Molly stood, uncertain and confused, then went into the kitchen on the pretext of checking the bread baking in the oven. Her mind was whirling. How dare Donna say she had been invited to come here! She had never invited any of Aunt Dora's family to come visit, much less Donna, whose contempt for her was most obvious of all. She doubted she had exchanged a dozen words with her cousin in the last five years. Donna wanted Adam. She had made that plain enough. A cold, icy dread started forming around Molly's heart as she remembered the lipstick she found in the bedroom of his apartment. *Had he been meeting Donna while on his trips to the city? Had he asked her to come here?*

Donna was entertaining the men with a story about mutual acquaintances in the city. She was cheerful and witty, and Adam seemed to be enjoying her company. She had slipped off the bulky snowmobile suit, looking slim and beautiful leaning against the mantel, her tight-fitting coral knit slacks and sweater a perfect foil for her figure and silver hair.

Molly grabbed up a cloth and went to wipe up the puddle of water made by Donna's boots.

"Here, let me do that." Adam tried to take the cloth from her hand.

"I'll do it." Her voice was tighter than she intended, and she kept the cloth in her hand, refusing to relinquish it. Almost glaring at him she added, "Lunch is almost ready."

He frowned, then shrugged his shoulders and joined the others. *He didn't even kiss me when he came in,* Molly thought angrily.

She poured the coffee for lunch and reluctantly admitted her cousin had an unfailing gift for monopolizing male attention. Her husky overtones, her tinkling laughter, the men's lower voices, all joined together. Molly was silent during the meal, speaking only when necessary.

"Your wife's a good cook, Adam. Pretty and a good cook. You can't beat that combination." Patrick was a diplomat, Molly decided.

"She is pretty, isn't she?" Adam's face creased with a smile. He tried to hold her eyes with his, but Molly looked away.

"Molly is a good cook," Donna chimed in. "She used to live with us, you know. Mama always said if Molly opened a restaurant in Anchorage, she would make a mint!"

"It would be a terrible waste to hide all that beauty in the kitchen." Patrick's voice had a slightly critical tone.

"I didn't mean to hide her. You know that, Pat, darling. I just meant she is such a good cook it's a shame to waste all that talent."

Molly got up from the table to serve the dessert and thought her churning stomach was going to betray her, but her self-discipline and pride came to her rescue.

Seating herself again, she looked directly at Patrick. "Tell us about your trip to Australia." Her voice didn't betray her, thank God, and she had, at least, got the attention away from Donna.

The remainder of the dinner conversation was lost to Molly as her mind turned over the possibility that Adam hadn't wanted to be alone with her. That thought was only a step away from the speculation that Donna was the woman he loved and he would not have insisted on consummating their marriage without her invitation.

If the two large cases Donna had brought with her were any indication, she had come prepared for a long stay. Her clothes took up more than half of Molly's wardrobe. The perfumes and cosmetics that she used to retain her clear, soft skin dominated Molly's dressing table. Her belongings were strewn around the room which had literally taken on her personality.

In the afternoon she changed from slacks to a long, plaid wool skirt which she paired with a long-sleeved, high-necked sweater. Looking elegant and sensual she curled herself up in the big chair with a magazine and Adam's transistor radio after the men went to Adam's room to look over his work.

Molly stayed in the kitchen. She wanted to stay as far away from her cousin as possible. She cleaned shelves and rearranged the supply cabinet. The work absorbed a couple of hours and her jumbled thoughts were no closer together when she stopped than when she started.

Donna sauntered in to lean against the counter and watch her. Molly knew she had something to say and braced for the ridicule that was sure to come.

"Adam said he would do anything to get his hands on Uncle Charlie's files." Molly glanced at her cousin and saw malice in her eyes. "Guess Uncle Charlie thought that would be the only way he could get a husband for you."

"What do you mean?" Molly's hands stopped their movement. Her cousin's blue eyes stared at her arrogantly, and the corners of her pink lips tilted.

"Adam told all of us, the gang at the club that is, that he would have to marry you, but he said he was going to get more out of it than just the files. We made some bets, and if you know Adam like I do, you know he can't resist a dare. He bet our friends at the club that he would have you in bed in less than a month." She paused, then added a contemptuous little laugh. "He intends to collect six thousand dollars on that bet." Her voice took on a confidential tone. "I wanted to warn you, Molly. I don't like you very much, but after all, you are my cousin. I think it was kind of stinking of Adam. After all, you're not wise in the ways of a man like him."

Molly stared at her disbelievingly. She felt sickened. Humiliation made her stomach heave. She could feel the betraying tears prickling at her eyes and turned away.

"Who told you about the will, Donna?" She used every effort she possessed to keep her voice calm.

"Adam—who else? He said if he didn't marry you, the files would be destroyed, and Mama would have control of your money and have to look after you for five years." Her voice took on a dreamy quality. "He knew I'd wait for him." She looked at Molly's drawn white face and pressed on. "He told me it was only for a year and if I loved him, I should be willing to wait that long."

Molly was shaken to the core. Along with her anguish, she felt a white hot fury. She wanted to strike that mocking mouth, but not even that satisfaction would have wiped out the pain Donna had caused her, or the truth of her statements for that matter. If ever she wished herself dead, it was at this moment.

Satisfied that she had accomplished what she had come here to do, Donna sauntered back to her chair by the fire and picked up her magazine.

Stunned by the obvious truth of her cousin's words, and the betrayal of the man to whom she had given her heart and body, Molly numbly went to the bedroom. After closing the door softly behind her and making sure the connecting bathroom door was firmly closed, she collapsed on the bed. A noise like pounding surf was reverberating through her head. Her limbs shook as if with a fever as reaction set in. Her tortured senses were unable to believe Adam would play such a cruel trick. She choked on a thousand unanswered questions. The humiliation came up in the form of a lump in her throat which she thought she would never be able to swallow. The shame of remembering how she had asked him, had almost begged him to come to bed with her, drew her to her feet, and a wave of weakness set her swaying against the bedpost. She looked at herself in the mirror.

"You fool!" she said aloud. "You dumb, stupid fool!"

She drew on all the courage she had and refused to give in to a storm of weeping. It may have been an inherited pride which decreed that humiliation must be borne with head held high. Whichever it was, her courage or her pride, she looked far from downcast when she opened the door and went out of the room.

Holding herself aloof from all that Donna had said, she spent the next few hours in the kitchen. The first hour or so was taken up with cleaning. She washed the cabinets and counter, scrubbed the wall behind the big range,

161

washed all the globes on the gaslamps, and polished them until they shone. When the kitchen was spotlessly clean, she started baking. She made cookies and cake, the kind Jim liked best, rolled out a half a dozen pie crusts and put them in the freezer, then started a meat pie baking in the range oven. With the kitchen neat once again she put on her parka and went out into the cold, crisp air to bring in more wood for the range. It was totally dark now. The short winter days brought the darkness long before dinner time.

Dog was in the yard and ran to meet her, wagging his tail and making a circle of tracks in the snow. She almost broke her stony composure at his show of affection. Keeping her mind in the safe chamber of suspension, she threw a few sticks for him to chase, patted his head, and returned to the house.

After dumping her armload of wood in the box by the range, she took off her heavy parka and was hanging it on the hook, when Patrick and Adam came into the kitchen. She turned to face them.

"What's the matter?" Adam stopped short. "Aren't you feeling well?"

"I'm all right." Beyond his shoulder she could see Donna approaching and for an instant closed her eyes. Then she turned her head and forced her stiff lips to stretch into a smile. "Why wouldn't I be?"

Adam got out glasses and bottles and mixed drinks. *Entertaining is easy for him,* Molly thought resentfully. Donna kept up a flow of amusing chatter. Molly was able to maintain her composure; the shock of the betrayal had blocked out every emotion and she felt herself in perfect control. She was determined to be the master of her own actions.

Afterward, she didn't know how she got through the rest of the evening. Only her strength of character kept the inner misery from surging up and boiling out of her.

When Adam came to her, she looked at him with vacant eyes.

"Would you like a drink, Molly mine?" he asked softly, intimately.

She shook her head. *Deceit comes to him as naturally as breathing,* she thought. A mask of politeness moved over her face.

"Excuse me. I'll get the dinner on."

For a long while she didn't have to speak or look at any of them. Donna was at the end of the room. The "personal message" program was being broadcast for the second time that day and she was listening and laughing with the two men about the advice given Mrs. Watson regarding her lumbago and the report of the Johnson's groceries being left at the wrong stop.

"I can't believe it!" she exclaimed. "Imagine, having everyone in the North knowing about your lumbago!"

"That's how Adam knew to meet us at the tracks," Patrick told her. "He heard it on this program."

"Is that true, Adam?" Donna turned the full force of her blue eyes on him. "You knew I'd be there with Patrick?"

"No. They just said visitors were coming."

The murmur of their voices surged over and around Molly, although she was near enough to join in the conversation if she had wished to; but the words they spoke were inaudible to her numbed senses. An air of unreality settled over her. With the perfectly groomed table prepared, and the food on it, she approached the others and told them that dinner was ready.

She served the meal calmly and efficiently, exchanging pleasantries with Patrick, asking him about the food in Australia. Her glance passed indifferently over Adam. He and Donna talked together about some person unknown to her. One time Donna's voice directed a question to her.

She looked in her direction, and her face suddenly blurred, so she turned away and ignored her.

Patrick helped with the cleanup. She would never know what they talked about. The time seemed to go terribly fast and they were finished.

"You've worked enough for today, Molly. Come sit by me." Adam beckoned to her.

She shook her head, not bothering to answer. A frown came over his face and he came toward her.

"What's the matter with you? What's wrong?"

"Nothing's wrong, I'm going to bed." She started toward her room. He grabbed her arm and turned her around.

"You're not going to bed!" he grated. "We have guests."

She stood still, looking down at the hand holding her arm. A shudder of repulsion shook her.

"Your guests. Not mine."

"You said you didn't mind Pat coming and Donna is your cousin," he hissed at her.

"I'll prepare their food, but that's all. Let me go!" Her voice was deadly quiet.

He released her arm. "I don't understand you."

"No," she said, "I guess you don't." She left him looking after her with a look of astonishment on his face.

In her room she fumbled in the dark until her fingers felt the familiar lamp and turned it on. Her dazed eyes took in the articles on her table and the clothing strung around the room. She clicked off the lamp, not wanting to see these things, and undressed in the dark. She found her gown under her pillow, slipped into it, and crawled into bed. Her body was weary and her head throbbed. Her troubled mind whirled and she sought the sweet oblivion of sleep. Worn out by the emotional upheaval she had been through she immediately sank into a deep sleep.

She awoke and sat up in bed. The illuminated dial on

her watch told her morning was several hours away. The events of the day before were clear in her mind. Knowing who was sleeping beside her, and not wanting to look at her, she kept her eyes averted and slipped out from under the covers. The air in the dark room was icy cold. Hastily she reached for her flashlight then donned jeans and a flannel shirt. She brushed her hair back, secured it with a rubber band, and left the room. The fire had burned down in the cooking range and the big log in the fireplace was almost used up. She shivered as she tugged the fire screen aside to poke at the coals on the grate. After selecting several small logs from the woodbox she carefully piled them on the burning coals and replaced the screen.

The house was unnaturally quiet. She cocked her head to one side and listened. Suddenly it occurred to her: the clock on the mantel was still. Aiming the beam of her light on the clock she found the glass door of the clock case was open and the pendulum had been removed. She replaced the pendulum, wound the clock, and started the pendulum swaying. The familiar ticking was comforting in the quiet room.

She stoked up the fire in the kitchen range and made coffee in the granite pot. Cupping her cold hands around the steaming cup she sat in the chair close to the fire and leaned forward to soak in the heat. The flickering flames cast a cozy glow around the dark room. The clock on the mantel struck five times. It would be awhile yet before the unwanted people in her home would be up and around.

She began to tremble and picked up the afghan from the couch and wrapped it around her shoulders. She rocked gently. The firelight threw her shadow on the wall and she watched it, not thinking or feeling, just rocking. The kindling snapped and popped and the flames spread to the larger logs and flared.

She got up, walking carefully, like someone in great

pain, and refilled her coffee cup. *They could keep love,* she thought, as she sat down again. *It wasn't worth the price.*

She tried to think of her father, tried to remember how happy he had made her when he brought her here to this house, but her thoughts kept straying. With a jerk she would drag them back from the forbidden territory, but back they would go as soon as she relaxed her restraint.

It was very odd to be sitting here, making plans to leave. From the very first moment she had known she would be leaving. Her pride warred endlessly with common sense even as pain stirred in her stomach. It hurt her. *Oh, God, how it hurt!* She would have done anything in the world for him . . . anything. It didn't seem that all this had really happened to her. How could her father have made such a ghastly mistake in judging a man's character? He would understand that she was doing what she had to do. She would go to Herb Belsile and tell him she couldn't accept the terms of the will. Tim-Two would look after the house until she could return.

She leaned forward and looked out the window. The light was definite now and the old Indian was coming toward the house. He made no sign that he was surprised to see her up, but stoically went about his chores of refueling the range and the fireplace. She poured him a cup of coffee. He sat at the trestle table. When he was finished, he nodded and went out.

At the first stirrings from the bedroom Molly rose and started breakfast; first setting the table and then slicing the bacon. She was deep in thought when a hand descended on her shoulder and swung her around. Adam stood there.

His eyes searched her face and his black brows drew together, but his expression held no terror for her. Suddenly his face changed and his eyes smiled into hers.

"Did you miss me last night as much as I missed you?"

She raised one hand then let it fall despairingly. She shrugged her shoulders and looked at him with dull eyes.

He seemed startled as though he had expected her to say or do something.

"Molly?" The silence lengthened after his voice died away. He made a grimace of displeasure.

She shrugged her shoulders again wearily and attempted to turn away. He yanked her arm and pulled her up close against him. She stood passive in his embrace. A wave of anger hit him and his mouth came down hard on hers, parting her lips and forcing her head back. His hands roamed over her, cupping her hips and holding them tightly against him. She made no protest and no response. When he lifted his head to look at her, she unhurriedly pushed herself away from him, and at that moment Patrick came into the room.

"Morning, Molly. Sleep the headache away?"

She nodded and gave him a half smile. "How many eggs, Patrick?" she asked quietly.

"However many you fix old Adam. I'm not as big as he is, but I eat as much." If he noticed any tension between them, he was ignoring it.

Adam sat at the table and Molly poured coffee. Patrick kept up a constant chain of chatter for a while, then fell silent because he wasn't getting much response from either of them. After serving the breakfast, Molly sat in her chair by the hearth and picked up her knitting.

Unconsciously she started to knit, then it dawned on her . . . she was knitting the sweater for Adam. Slowly she removed the needles and placed them on the table beside the chair and started unraveling the almost finished garment, rolling the yarn into a ball. She rocked as she pulled the soft wool, her fingers carefully winding the yarn. Adam came and stood over her, watching, then turned on his heel and went into his room.

Patrick brought his coffee cup and sat in the chair opposite her. She glanced at him and went on with her work. The thought drifted across her mind that this friend of

Adam's was nice and she could like him if things had been different. *I'll never get the chance to know him now, and he'll despise me when he can no longer use the files.*

Donna came out of Molly's room. She was wearing a white woolly robe and big fluffy lamb's wool slippers. Her silver hair was brushed back and held with a blue ribbon. She was plainly in a bad mood.

"I've never been so cold in all my life," she said crossly, coming to stand close to the fire. "Well . . . do you serve coffee or not?" Her question was directed to Molly.

She sat as if she hadn't heard.

"I'll get it, and don't be such a grouch, Donna." Patrick got up.

As he was speaking the clock on the mantel started striking the hour. Donna turned, her face a mask of fury.

"I hate striking clocks," she grated. "I stopped that damn thing last night and I meant for it to stay stopped!" She yanked open the glass door of the clock case, jerked off the swaying pendulum, and threw it into the blazing fire.

Molly let out a cry and rushed to get the iron poker. Frantically she raked the burning coals until she had pulled the small disc and stem out of the flames. She raked it out onto the stone hearth and looked at it, her head bent.

"That was a rotten thing to do, Donna!" Patrick was angry and it showed in his voice.

"I hate clocks and she knows it. She just started it again to spite me," she said hatefully, not one bit put off by Patrick's anger.

"That's no excuse! You're a guest here."

"Guest? Adam's guest, not hers. She'd poison me if she could!"

Patrick knelt down beside Molly. "I don't know as I would blame her," he muttered. He took the poker from Molly's hand, returned it to the rack, and picked up the

168

piece of metal, shifting it from one hand to the other as it cooled. "It isn't damaged, Molly," he said reassuringly.

Her face was white and the violet eyes, surrounded with dark circles, were bright with tears. She took the disc from him and put it in her pocket.

"Thank you," she whispered, and sat back down in the rocker.

"I don't know how Adam can stand this godforsaken place!" Donna hugged herself with her arms. "That bathroom is positively primitive."

Patrick stood looking from one to the other; Molly rocking and winding the yarn, Donna prancing around the room in a temper. He had seen Molly smile only once or twice since they had been here and the relationship between her and Adam certainly wasn't as he had been led to believe it was. As for Donna, he had seen dozens like that bitch and would never have brought her, but for her being Molly's cousin. After seeing the difference between the two of them, it seemed strange Molly would invite her. Suddenly it hit him! *How stupid can I be? The blond bombshell is still after Adam and she thinks the country cousin is no competition! But if I'm any judge of old Adam . . .*

"I suggest you get your own coffee and sit down, Donna," he said coolly.

"You don't have to be so nasty about it, Patrick. You may be used to living like a peasant, but I'm not!" She flounced into the kitchen and looked disgustedly at the big granite coffeepot.

Patrick stood uncertainly. He didn't want to leave Molly at the mercy of this cat. He wasn't sure, but something was very wrong here. Molly seemed to be in a sort of daze. She couldn't be like this all the time—an emotionless shell of a girl! She wasn't at all the picture he got from Robert and Aunt Flo. He wondered if he should talk to Adam about it.

169

Tim-Two came in the back door. Donna gave a shudder of revulsion when she saw him. He looked about the room then walked to Adam's door, opened it and went in, closing it behind him.

Molly could hear the murmur of voices, then what appeared to be a curse word in Adam's voice. Tim-Two came out of the room and toward Molly, stopped in front of her, and said one word.

"Dog."

Molly understood the urgency in the one word. Alarm filled her and she got to her feet.

"What's the matter with Dog?" she asked shrilly.

Adam came out of the bedroom putting on his parka. He went to the gun rack, lifted out the rifle, and checked the load. Biting her lip to keep back hysteria Molly ran after Tim-Two, grabbing her coat from the peg as she fled out the kitchen door.

Adam was shouting at her. "Stay in the house, Molly!"

Paying him no mind, she ran on and caught up with Tim-Two as he rounded the shed. She took one swift look and her steps faltered. Dog was lying in the snow behind the shed. She ran to him and dropped to her knees beside him. The impact of what had happened began to hammer in her brain. The snow was red with Dog's blood. His eyes were rolled back in his head and he was gasping for breath.

"Dog! Dog!" Dimly Molly heard her own anguished voice.

At the sound of her voice Dog tried to lift his head and focus his eyes, but the effort was too much for him and his big head sank down on the snow.

"Don't die. Please don't die!" Dog opened his eyes and tried to see the owner of the dear and familiar voice.

"Don't die, Dog," she pleaded. "I'll have no one!" Hiding her face in the soft fur of his neck, she talked to him beseechingly.

"Molly!" Hands were lifting her up. "You'll always

have someone. You'll have me." There was an agonizing note in Adam's voice.

A great roaring noise was in her ears; she swayed and would have collapsed if the hands had not held her. About to cross the thin line into hysteria, she turned on him and jerked herself away.

"Get away from me," she gasped, and then, with rising hysteria, "Oh, God! You're going to kill him!"

"I've got to, Molly, can't you see that?" His hands were reaching for her, trying to hold her.

A thin, shrill scream tore itself from her throat. She brought her hand up and tried to claw him. His hands held her arms pinioned to her sides.

"You've taken everything," she screamed at him. "Still you're not satisfied! You'd kill my dog! My dog, the only thing left in the world that I love and the only thing that loves me!"

Adam knew he couldn't reach her and reason with her through her hysteria. He stood helplessly for a moment and looked at her. Her face was deathly white and the dark-rimmed eyes were bright and darted wildly about. He shoved her toward Patrick who had come up beside him.

"Get her in the house and keep her there," he said harshly.

She burst into tearing, retching sobs and flung herself into Patrick's arms. He scooped her up and carried her to the house. It seemed as if the dam had finally burst. The emotional stress of the last day and night was finding release in the rush of tears that spilled out of her eyes and flooded down over her cheeks.

He had just sat her down in the house and closed the door when the sound of the rifle shot reached them. Molly clutched him and he held her tightly until the hard sobs ceased shaking her.

"Molly," he whispered in her ear. "Adam did the only

171

humane thing to do. He put the poor beast out of his misery. He'd been in a fight with a bear, or maybe a wolf, and only managed to drag himself home. He would have been dead before night. You wouldn't want him to lie there all day and suffer." He tried to look into her face. "Surely you understand."

"Well, I'll say one thing for her," Donna's grating voice broke the silence of the room. "She sure knows how to play up a good scene. Good riddance, if you ask me. That dog smelled like a pigsty!"

"Shut up, Donna!" Patrick's patience with Donna was almost at an end.

Quiet now, Molly wanted desperately to be alone. She lifted her head and wiped her eyes with the back of her hand.

"Thank you, Patrick." Her voice barely reached him.

She left him and walked slowly to the door of her room. She closed it behind her and leaned her weight against it as though to keep all of them out. Her disjointed thoughts whirled around in her brain. She must leave! She must get away from these people. A sudden sense of purpose sent her limbs into action, but how could she go and where could she go? She looked at her watch—if she were to leave at once . . . but . . . supposing he saw her and tried to stop her? Supposing he . . .

Adam had come into the house. She could hear his voice and the soft purring voice of her cousin. She never wanted to see either of them again as long as she lived! It had been a cruel, bitter lesson she had learned. She would never, no never, love anything again, she vowed. She had loved her mother, she had loved her father, she had loved this house, and she had loved Dog. She had loved . . . him. They all had been taken away from her!

When Adam and Patrick were settled into their work in the study, she would leave the house. It shouldn't be to difficult to slip out the kitchen door and walk away toward the rail lines. If she could make it to the tracks by the time the train for Anchorage passed, she would be on her way to Herb Belsile. Now that her mind was made up, there were things to be done. She changed from her jeans to heavy wool slacks and pulled on a sweater over her shirt. She lay out her fur mittens and thermal socks. She put what cash money she had and her checkbook in the pocket of her snowmobile suit and zipped it shut. She wished she dared take the snowmobile, but the noise when she started it would alert Adam.

Molly looked about the room she had always kept so tidy, and made a grimace at the disorder. Her cousin's belongings were everywhere. Suddenly the entire weight of her wretchedness hit her and she could hardly wait to leave this room, this house, where she had been so happy and where she had felt the blackest despair.

She heard Adam and Patrick go to her father's room, then the familiar sounds as they began their work. Hurriedly she dressed in the warm clothing she had selected and put on her snow boots. With wool stocking cap and mittens in hand, she went to the door and listened for sounds of her cousin moving about in the kitchen. She could hear music. She hoped Donna was curled up in the chair with the transistor radio. Cautiously she opened the door. With relief she saw Donna sitting in the chair with her back to the kitchen.

Molly walked softly to the back door and let herself out into the cold winter day.

CHAPTER FOURTEEN

Walking straight into the woods from the back door Molly circled the house, and headed in the general direction of the railroad tracks. She figured she had an hour and a half to walk the two miles. There was plenty of time to reach the tracks before the train came through. She hadn't gone far, however, until she wished she had brought her snowshoes, but they had been on the porch and she hadn't wanted to take the risk of being seen to get them. She walked as fast as she could in the deep snow, trying to pick the places where the snow was hard enough to hold her light weight.

She passed the clearing where the helicopter landed and noticed the first small intermittent snowflakes. She looked around with worried eyes and tried to walk faster. Within fifteen minutes flakes were falling—huge, fluffy, and thick. Several times she blundered into deep drifts and floundering through them came near to exhausting herself. She dared not stop to rest and consoled herself by thinking she would rest when she got to the tracks.

Doggedly she kept going, putting one foot in front of the other. Every step was taking her farther away from the sneering face of her cousin Donna and the deceitful opportunist she had married. She had been blind, stupid, and gullible to allow him to arouse her unmanageable emotions to the point where she had asked him . . . she had actually asked him to come to bed with her! She had not thought it possible to experience such humiliation and despair as she had felt when Donna told her he had actually made bets with his friends about getting her to bed! How he would enjoy telling them that she had asked him! She would never forgive him for that or for telling Donna about her father's will.

She looked at her watch and was surprised to see she had been walking for over an hour. She should be coming to the tracks any time now. The new snow was getting deep and it was harder to stay out of the drifts. She was tired and hoped it wouldn't be much farther. She staggered and scrambled out of snowdrift after snowdrift. She had a stabbing pain in her side, but she dared not stop. The time for the train to pass was getting short.

Looking around her she began to feel a little afraid. She tried to reason out where she was, to recall how far she had to go. A frightening thought came to her. When she had crawled out of one of the drifts, had she veered off in a slanting direction? Could she be lost? She was frightened now, so frightened that for a moment she thought she was going to be sick from the fear that cramped her stomach.

Wanting to look at her watch and yet afraid to, she hurried on. Coming to where a large tree was uprooted and turned on its side, she sat down on the big trunk to get her breath. She knew for sure, now, she was lost. She had been walking for more than two hours. There would not be more than an hour of daylight left. A pain of terror shot through her. She could very well die out here!

Should she try and follow her own tracks back to the house? The new snow had probably filled them by now. Common sense told her she had missed the train and should turn back. Even if she could find her way back . . . to go back in defeat, to have Donna sneer, and . . . him know she was a prisoner in her own home? Again pride warred with common sense, with all her father had taught her about survival in the wilderness. She wouldn't go back! She got to her feet and pressed on, her eyes straining ahead to catch a glimpse of just anything but snow and trees. Thinking of nothing, she put one foot ahead of the other and trudged onward.

It was colder. The snow whipped about her and she thought of calling out. But she didn't call out, the thought went out of her mind as another pushed its way in. Did it matter so much if she did die out here? Would anyone care? Really, who would care besides Jim and Evelyn? Tim-Two would miss her, but he would still stay on in his cabin. It wouldn't change his life. She would never deliberately let it happen she thought, but if it did . . .

Coming to another large overturned tree, she sat down to rest, and let the large trunk shelter her from the wind. She was so tired. She was sure she had never been this tired before. She lifted up one mittened hand and let it fall. All her strength was gone. Her mind wandered to the good things; to her father and to Jim, who loved Evelyn and his boys. It was too late for her to find someone like Jim. She sat there for a long time and let the sweet numbness drift over her.

Did she hear her father calling? He always called her like that.

"Mol . . . ly." He must be coming for her, but she would like to stay here and sleep. It was nice and warm here.

"Mol . . . ly!" He called again. She opened her eyes and saw him coming toward her. She tried to get up, but he was running and she didn't have time to get to her feet.

"Dad! Oh, Dad!"

"Molly, darling! Oh, my love, are you all right?" He grabbed her roughly into his arms and pressed his warm cheek against her cold one. "Oh, Molly," he groaned unsteadily. "Thank God, we found you!"

"Dad . . ." Her voice was barely audible.

Adam's frantic, questioning eyes sought those of the Indian beside him.

"She thinks I'm her father!"

"Mind wanders, when lost," the Indian replied.

"We've got to get her back to the snowmobile." Adam swung her up in his arms and staggered through the snow.

It was completely dark, now, and Adam, carrying his precious load, followed the Indian. The terror that they would find her too late was replaced with a feeling of thankfulness and a promise . . .

In her semiconscious state Molly knew her father was taking her to a warm, safe place and she wanted to talk to him, she had to tell him . . . she had to tell someone!

"I can't go back there. Donna is there . . . and she told me about . . . him."

Adam caught his breath and shifted her in his arms so her lips were closer to his ear.

"You didn't know him like you thought you did, Dad." Her soft voice quavered and tears squeezed out from under the tightly closed lids. "He made bets with his friends about me! About going . . . going to bed with me . . . and I loved him and asked him . . . to . . ." Her lips trembled and her face contorted into a mask of utter despair.

"Oh, my God!" Adam's eyes misted over and he dropped down on his knees in the snow and rocked her in his arms.

"Darling, darling, don't cry!" Her face against his was cold and wet. He kissed her tears and tried to warm her cold face with his lips. He unzipped the neck of his suit and pressed her face against his neck and looked up at the Indian who had stopped and stood with his back to them.

He got clumsily to his feet with the girl in his arms. Sudden rage at what had been done to her filled and consumed him. He barely felt her weight as he plowed through the snowdrifts to the snowmobile.

The beam from the Indian's light found the machine where they had left it on the high ground when his native instinct had told him she had turned off in the direction where they found her. The Indian got into the back of the machine and held out his arms for the girl. Adam wrapped her securely in a blanket and reluctantly handed her over to him.

The big light on the machine picked out a path through the timber. Adam's temper cooled as the wind hit his face. What a blind, stupid fool he had been not to have seen the change that came over her immediately after her cousin arrived. He'd been so engrossed in discussing the work with Patrick that he hadn't noticed anything was wrong until she announced she was going to bed just after dinner. Was it only last night? It seemed he had lived a lifetime in the few hours he and the Indian had been searching for her.

God, how he had hated to shoot that dog! He could understand now her unreasonable attitude and why she had lashed out at him with such hate and venom. He didn't think he had ever had anything depress him as much as the sight of her kneeling there in the snow begging the dog not to die! At that moment he had made up his mind to get Patrick and Donna back to Anchorage as soon as he could so he could be alone with her again. He had gone to the study to prepare some work for Patrick to take back to the apartment. She was gone when they came out of the bedroom, but thinking she had gone to the cabin to talk to Tim-Two, he hadn't been alarmed. Later, when the Indian came in and said he hadn't seen her, the knot that tied itself up in his stomach at the thought of her being out there alone was still painful to him. Thank God for the Indian and his knowledge of the woods!

They came out of the timber and into the yard. He stopped the machine beside the porch and climbed out.

"Thank you, my friend, thank you," he said as he lifted Molly from Tim-Two's arms. The Indian got out and silently walked toward his cabin.

178

The door opened and the light from the house splayed out onto the porch. Adam carried Molly into the house and gently lowered her down on the couch.

"You found her." Donna lazily got up from the chair, tossing her magazine aside. "I knew you would. She intended for you to find her."

Adam straightened and his dark eyes found her face. She almost recoiled from the look he gave her.

"Get your things out of my wife's room." His voice was deadly quiet and his lips barely moved as he spoke.

Donna looked dumbfounded.

"Now!" he said. "Pack them up. You're leaving in the morning and you'll sleep in the other room tonight."

"What has she said to you?" Donna stammered. "She's lying if she said anything . . ."

The murderous look he turned on her shut off her words and she closed her mouth.

"When you've packed, go into the other room and close the door. I don't want to see your face again tonight, or I won't be responsible . . ."

A look of pure fright came into Donna's face and she hurriedly left the room.

Adam looked toward the other person standing quietly by.

"If the weather clears, can you fly her out of here in the morning?"

"I sure can, old man. I'll get her out of here if I have to take her out on her broomstick."

"I'll appreciate it. Would you mind taking the snowmobile to the shed?"

"Not at all." Patrick plucked his coat from the peg on the wall.

Adam knelt and removed Molly's wool cap. He smoothed back the hair from the tear-streaked face. His heart filled with such an overpowering protectiveness that he just sat looking at her for a moment before taking off

179

her snow boots. He held her bare foot in his hand. It was warm to his touch, a good sign. He was thankful for the full-length zipper on her suit that allowed him to lift her out of it easily. She would have died out there if it hadn't been for this warm suit. He wrapped her in the afghan from the back of the couch and covered her with the blanket from the snowmobile.

Patrick came in and stoked up the fire in the range. He put the coffeepot on and got out the makings for sandwiches. Adam sat beside Molly and Patrick grinned to himself. Donna was slamming things around in Molly's room as she packed the expensive wardrobe she had brought to impress Adam. Hearing this, Patrick's grin turned to soft laughter. He wouldn't have missed hearing Adam tell her off for anything! He took a sandwich and a mug of coffee and put them on the table beside Adam.

Adam glanced up as if reluctant to take his eyes from Molly.

"Thanks. Do you think I should wake her? She hasn't had a thing to eat all day."

"I'd let her sleep until you can get her in her own bed."

"I guess you're right." Adam picked up the coffee and sipped it slowly, his clouded black eyes still on his wife's face.

"You've finally got it, haven't you, old man?" Patrick put his hand on Adam's shoulder. Adam didn't answer and he said quite seriously, "I don't blame you, old buddy. I only wish I'd seen her first." Adam looked at him then. He grinned and went back to the kitchen.

Later, when Donna left Molly's room, Adam went there. He turned up the light and went over the room, making sure every sign that her cousin had been there was removed. He remade the bed with clean sheet blankets and rearranged Molly's few simple toilet articles on the dressing table. He took out the warm nightgown he had dressed her in once before and thought about how open and honest she was. How unaffected! *God, how lucky I am, or how lucky I was. Is it too late? Has the feeling she had for me been killed by my stupidity and her cousin's vindictiveness? How many years lay ahead? Years without her! My life was only an empty shell; a man without love, without a meaningful life, until I met her.*

Molly slept for hours. The emotional strain, the long hike in the deep snow, and the fact she had very little food in the last forty-eight hours had taken a toll of her strength. She was exhausted and slept on, unaware of the gaunt-faced man who kept vigil beside her bed.

When she awoke, she lay for a minute with her eyes closed. She was warm and she knew she was in her own bed. Finally she lifted her lids. Her eyes swung around to the man sitting in the chair beside the bed. He sat up and leaned forward when he became aware she was awake.

"Oh no, not . . . you!" she gasped, and turned her head away. Weak tears filled her eyes and ran down her cheeks. Her lips trembled helplessly.

Adam got down onto his knees beside the bed and tried to turn her face toward him.

"Don't turn away from me, darling. I've waited all night for you to wake up." His voice was pleading, but the shame and humiliation she had felt came surging back and she resisted the hand on her cheek. "Darling, she's gone. Donna is gone. Patrick took her back in the plane this morning . . . please, look at me!"

A soft cloth wiped the tears from her eyes and she turned her head and looked into his face. She didn't know what she expected to see, but what she did see was pleading eyes that were slightly bloodshot from lack of sleep and a gaunt, worried face with cheeks that were dark with a day's growth of beard.

"Darling, she's gone," he repeated. "I wanted to tell you the moment you woke up that the things she told you were not true. Please believe me, love! You told me last night what she had said to you, why you took such a risk to get away from me."

Molly's tearful eyes focused on his face. He seemed so sincere, but she wouldn't trust him a second time! He would break her heart again! She closed her eyes tightly to shut out the picture of the face so close to hers. She felt him draw her close and she was too weak to resist. He buried his face in the curve of her neck and his whispered words went on.

"Let me talk to you, Molly. Don't shut me out." His voice was emotional, not at all like his usual voice. "Once, years ago, when I was young and thought of myself as something special, I made bets with some of the other fellows at the club. But not for years, and certainly not about you! I've never mentioned you to anyone at the club. I'll swear to it! You can't believe I would do something like that, Molly. Look at me and tell me!"

He shook her gently and she opened her eyes. She wanted to believe him. Oh, how she wanted to believe him! Her eyes filled again and her mouth trembled as the doubts came back to her mind.

"You told her about the . . . will. Asked her to . . . wait for you."

"Sweetheart." He kissed the tear wet eyes. "I never told her anything. Her mother was entitled to read the will and probably did. I expected that. I haven't talked to your cousin but one time since I knew about Charlie's will."

"She . . . she was in your apartment." Molly persisted.

"Our apartment," he corrected gently. "Yes, the last time I went to Anchorage she saw me at the airport and she knew I was at the apartment. She came up and inquired about you. She didn't stay five minutes. I went up to see Dad and she asked to freshen up before she left because she had an important date. Ganson was with us the whole time, love."

Molly's mind was still troubled. He had explained everything so beautifully, yet he hadn't said the words she so much wanted to hear. He read the doubt still in her eyes and put his arms under and around her and hugged her desperately to him.

"Sweetheart." His voice was ragged in her ear. "I don't know what I'll do if you don't believe me! Remember our first night together? I was coming to you that night when you called out to me. That was the happiest night of my life, darling. You told me over and over that you loved me. Have I lost you, Molly mine? Have I?"

The words rang in Molly's ears. He had been coming to her! Her heart sang out and her arms went up and around his neck, giving him the answer he hoped for. He kissed her desperately and lovingly, going from her mouth to her eyes, to the curve of her neck, forgetting the day's growth of beard was scratching the soft skin of her face. Molly gloried in the hurt of his rough face against hers, and sought his mouth with her own trembling lips.

"Darling, I love you. I love you so." He murmured the magic words that set her heart aflame. "I knew I loved you even before that perfect night when you gave me the most precious thing a woman has to give a man. But now that I almost lost you . . ."

The happiness in Molly's heart cried out . . . *he loves me! Can it really be true?* Her desperate heart wanted to believe it was true. The black eyes were staring adoringly into hers. He was gentle now, the relief plain on his face, and she put her palms up to his rough cheeks and he turned his lips into them.

"I love you, Adam. Through it all I loved you. That was why I was so desperate."

The black eyes that could be so hard and cold were now warm and glowing and misted over as he hid his face against her breast. She felt him tremble as if with a chill and she pressed his dark head against her. His trembling ceased and he raised his dark head, trailing his lips across her cheek to her mouth. He rubbed her lips gently with his until he got just the degree of opening he desired and then he kissed her, earnestly and hungrily.

"I've something else I want to tell you, my darling."

"What could you tell me that's more important than this?" She held up her lips for another kiss.

He laughed softly and kissed her again, running his hand under the bedclothes and down over her breasts to her flat, sunken, empty stomach that was growling in protest.

"I'm going to have to get some food into you." He gently caressed the empty spot. "But, first, I want no secrets between us, so I'm going to tell you something."

She looked at him searchingly, suddenly frightened that what he had to tell her would snatch away her happiness.

"You remember the first day I came here and Herb told you about your father's will?" She nodded. "Herb gave each of us a letter from your father. You took yours to the bedroom to read and I opened mine in the living room. My letter was a second will. It was dated after the one Herb probated and it was the valid legal will." Molly's face reflected her astonishment. "In the final will your father left all his files and charts, his notes and any other material connected with his work to me. He left the money to you with no strings attached. There was a letter attached to the will. In it he told me that if I found it impossible to abide by the conditions of the will Herb had read to us, or if either you or I found the other to be physically repulsive, I was to show the later will to Herb and have it probated. I thought about it, love, and I was tempted, but what Charlie counted on, happened. I had seen you! You came out of the bedroom and stood with so much pride in front of me and gave me your decision, I thought you were adorable and meant to have you for my own."

Molly eyed him disbelievingly. "You . . . didn't have to marry me to get the files?"

184

"No, pretty baby," he said with a laugh. "I didn't marry you to get the files. I married you because I wanted to. Because I didn't want you to get away from me before I had the chance to know you. To . . . find out if you could love me. I was pretty sure I would come to love you."

"You did?"

"Yes, I did." He kissed her.

"Remember the first time I tried to make love to you?" The color that came up in her cheeks told him she did. "After I had time to cool off I was glad you turned me down. I knew when you gave yourself to me it would be because you loved me. I haven't had much love, Molly. Only from Dad, and now from you. The only true friend I have is Patrick, and now he is going to have to go on another expedition alone." He laughed joyously at the look on her face and hugged her close. "You're not going to get away from me, Molly mine. I'm staying with you or taking you with me from now on. Patrick can do the field work and I'll stay at home with my wife and kids and take care of the paper work."

Molly couldn't believe she heard correctly. "You'll not be leaving at the end of the year?"

"No," he said emphatically. He rubbed her stomach gently. "Besides, you'll be pregnant by then and I'll have to stay home and rub your stomach and feel my son grow."

He watched the color come up her cheeks and flood her face. His eyes danced with devilry. He loved making her blush. She was adorable and she was . . . his!

Molly's arms reached out to him and wound around his neck, inviting his possession of her.

"Molly?" His voice questioned when he raised his lips from her clinging ones.

Her eyes told him the answer and he stood up, fingers working at the buttons on his shirt. Her eyes never left him as he hastily shed his clothing and lifted the blankets to slip in beside her. Her soft, white, bare body against his said she wanted him.

The old Indian slipped in the back door. Keeping his eyes away from the bedroom he stoked up the kitchen stove, put a big log on the already glowing coals of the fireplace, and silently went out again.

A week later Patrick came in the ski plane to take them to Anchorage to see Adam's father. A radiant Molly met him at the door. Her eyes sparkled with happiness. This was the girl he had expected to see the first time he came.

"Patrick, will you ever forgive me for the way I acted when you were here before?"

"I don't ever remember being here before, Mrs. Reneau." His blue eyes were merry with teasing. "You have a lovely wife, Mr. Reneau," he said to Adam. "May I kiss her?"

"You may not!" Adam firmly pulled Molly back against him, folded his arms around her, and planted a quick kiss beneath her ear. "Her kisses are spoken for—for the next forty years."

Later that day Molly and Adam walked hand in hand into the sitting room of his father's apartment. The old man was sitting in his same chair and watched them come toward him.

"Hello, Papa," Molly said and bent down to kiss his cheek.

"Hello, daughter, son." His eyes went to their interlaced fingers, then twinkled up to their eyes. "Sit down, sit down."

Adam pulled the big footstool up close to his father's chair as he always did for Molly, but today he sat down on it and pulled her down onto his lap.

"She loves me, Dad," Adam said with a kind of wonder in his voice.

"Well . . . ?"

"I love her," Adam said simply.

The old man laughed loudly. "So Charlie's plan worked, did it? I told him it would." He grinned broadly, his faded old eyes lighting up at the news he had sprung on them.

"You knew about the will?" Molly gasped.

"Sure did. Charlie and I talked about it."

A glance told Molly that Adam was as surprised as she was by this news.

"We—we came today to tell you," she stammered.

Robert Reneau settled back, enjoying the situation he had created. "Charlie came to see me before he made out the will. I've known Charlie Develon for thirty years. The doctors had given him about six months on the outside and he was worried about his girl. Of all the men he knew, son, he chose you to take care of his most precious possession. He wanted to get the two of you together and was planning to have you come and work with him when he returned from the expedition. He was sure you'd want her and love her once you met her." He paused to see what impact his words had made on them and smiled to see his son's arms tighten about his young wife. "He told me the plan and I thought it was a good one, but . . . I knew my son. Put the screws on him to force him to do something and he'll rebel, Charlie, I told him. So I persuaded him to make a second will giving my son a choice."

"Why, you old rascal!" Adam exclaimed. "I didn't know you even knew Charlie."

"How could you plan our lives like that? Why . . . we might not have even liked one another. Think of what the year would have been like for us if . . . you had been wrong!"

"But we weren't wrong. We were right." The old man interrupted Molly gleefully. "The plan worked."

"Yes, it sure did!" Molly said, and slipped her arms around her husband's neck.

When You Want A Little More Than Romance—

Try A Candlelight Ecstasy!

 Dell